I0546195

SPICE OF LIFE

Singapore Short Stories

RAYMOND HAN

Little Rocket Books

Copyright © Raymond Han 2013

All Rights Reserved

First published in 2013

Raymond Han has asserted his moral right to be identified as the author of the work.

This is a work of fiction.

All characters in this publication are fictitious and any resemblance to real persons, living or dead, is purely coincidental.

ISBN 978-981-07-7056-3

National Library Board, Singapore Cataloguing-in-Publication Data

Han, Raymond, 1958-

Spice of life : Singapore short stories / Raymond Han. – [Singapore] : [Little Rocket Books], 2013.

pages cm

ISBN : 978-981-07-7056-3 (paperback)

1. Teenagers – Singapore – Fiction. I. Title.

PR9570.S53

S823 -- dc23   OCN851681764

URL: www.raymondhan.net

Email: han.raymond@hotmail.com

Little Rocket Books, Singapore

Dedication

To my dearest Cindy, who has been the driving force in my journey to complete this my first collection of Singapore short stories.

Thank You!

To all my students, past and present, from the different government schools and also the private school, where I taught over the years from 1999 to 2012, for giving me the inspiration to continue this, at times, solitary pastime of mine – writing about the young in Singapore. In the short stories in this book, I have sprinkled insights into the lives of ordinary youngsters from different generations of modern Singapore.

About the Author

Raymond Han is a late baby boomer in Singapore. He has worked as a banker, an editor and a teacher.

After he left the banking sector, he found a second career teaching English Language to upper and lower secondary students in Victoria School, Montfort Secondary School, Greendale Secondary School and Hougang Secondary School.

Raymond also taught English at 'O' Level and General Paper to students in a private school for several years.

Contents

The story, Reflections, is set in the late sixties in Singapore.

Reflections

"Kai Ming! Kai Ming!" cracked his mother's voice.

"Have you finished pounding the chilli?"

She finally appeared at the doorway to the kitchen, having given up getting a reply from Kai Ming.

"What are you daydreaming about?" said she.

Kai Ming was lost in his own world, as usual. His mind was still throwing up the adventures of the Famous Five in the Enid Blyton book 'Five Go Adventuring Again' which he had read the night before. How he longed to be in England, having the adventure of his life. It was such fun, what with George, Anne, Julian, and Dick, not forgetting of course good old Tim, their pet dog. Kai Ming wasn't lonely in Singapore when he was with these guys. Their company kept him occupied most days when he wasn't outside playing. It was the only world he liked, though it was only make-believe.

1

Fiction. But it didn't matter to him. He was comfortable. He was satisfied and at peace with himself. It was only when he had to put away the book he was reading that he abruptly entered the mundane world again.

A slap on his shoulder put an end to his daydreaming. He was back in the real world again.

"Daydream! All you know is daydreaming," barked his mother.

"I...I..," was all Kai Ming could mutter.

Then his mother stopped her racket.

"My, my. What nice ground chilli you have done for me."

"I do declare this must be the best you have pounded so far."

Kai Ming had got used to his mother's whimsical mannerisms. He washed his hands and darted out of the kitchen into the living room. Home to him was a two-room HDB flat in Block 107 in Queenstown, the earliest public housing estate in the country. There was only one bedroom, into which crowded the whole family at bedtime. The kitchen was a narrow short passage, barely two metres in length, leading into the balcony where a long bamboo blind shielded the occupants from the direct rays of the sun while they were having their meals. Adjacent stood the toilet cum bathroom – a narrow cubicle with a water urn for bath use and a squatting pan at one end. The floor in the whole flat was all bare cement screed.

There was no grille gate attached to the front doorway. A cane chair, a foldable table and four stools dotted the spartan living room. Of course, there was the ubiquitous altar cabinet on which stood a statue of the Goddess of Mercy which his mother would talk to every morning, afternoon and night without fail. He could not understand how she could connect with the Goddess who was in another dimension. Day in and day out she would remind him to burn joss-sticks for the Goddess, and day in and day out he would find ways and means to avoid doing it.

His mother wanted him to talk to the Goddess. That wasn't the point. He was afraid she would answer him and he wasn't prepared for that situation, not yet, anyway. So it was with great reluctance that he had to burn joss-sticks to ask the Goddess to bless Father and Mother and Big Sister and him. He had no choice this time; his mother was standing behind him.

"Oh well, better luck next time," he thought to himself.

The family's only means of entertainment was a Rediffusion set blaring away from the wall where it was perched. The Rediffusion radio service had kept many a household entertained then. Mandarin programmes were unheard of at the time. The programmes which were broadcast were all in dialects. This service was one of the few 'luxuries' the typical Singapore household of the time could afford. Then every boy wore singlets. There were no jeans, no T-shirts and no McDonald's to speak of. The few games played by youngsters were 'cuti-cuti', 'five stones', 'hop-scotch', 'goli' and 'trading cards'.

This was the Singapore in which Kai Ming spent his childhood. This boy was very independent. He had no father to hover over him and control him because his father, being a sailor, was overseas most of the time. Kai Ming spent much of his free time outside the flat in the neighbourhood playing with his peers. His elder sister was a cashier at the Jurong Drive-In Cinema, a novelty at the time, having opened barely three months back. He had not been there before but had heard from his sister how big the screen was. Every night cars would queue all the way from the front gate to the main road several blocks away and the movies were always sold out.

"Kai Ming! Kai Ming!" his mother bellowed again.

Her plump figure gave backing to her loud voice. She had been father and mother to him most of his life as his father was never around. But still she had carried out her duties quite well. Kai Ming, though mischievous at times, never committed big sins like stealing and smoking.

Kai Ming poked his face into the kitchen.

3

"What is it this time, mother?"

"Kai Ming, tomorrow, we are visiting your Uncle Chiam. Do be on your best behaviour or I will give you some *kway teow* to eat when we get back."

Of course, by now Kai Ming was looking very squeamish indeed. He had 'eaten' lots of *kway teow* before and never once liked its taste. His legs still bore the cane marks left behind during the last 'meal'. He scampered off at once, out through the corridor, and up to the fifth storey landing where his *kakees* were waiting for him.

"Why are you late again?" asked Choon Huat.

"Eh, eh.. I had to help my mother pound the chilli," came the reply.

"*Aiyah*, don't let's waste time any more, we have to be on the hill by ten and we're already late," cried Juk.

Choon Huat and Juk were Kai Ming's best pals. The three of them were neighbours and also attended the same primary school – New Town Primary School – a ten-minute walk away from their block. But it was the school holidays and the school was closed.

Kai Ming was the tallest of the three. His lanky legs provided most of the support for his thin frame of a body. He had well-pressed hair which smelled of the Brylcreem he had applied. Just above his forehead, his hair trailed off into a neat 'curry puff' pattern. He wasn't much of a talker as he was reserved and shy. Choon Huat was the exact opposite. His mouth was like a machine gun – always shooting and never stopping. His bubbly, round face seemed to match his equally bubbly legs. He also had a 'curry puff' hairstyle.

Juk was the shortest of the trio. He had short straight hair. His cute adorable looks always managed to attract the attention of the *Ah Sohs* around the neighbourhood. They would come up to him and pinch his cheeks as if these were displayed for sale in a stall. Still, he wasn't ever mad with them.

In those days, in the late sixties, children did not have much pocket money. Most families were poor and the three were no different. Between the three of them, they only had fifteen cents. Still, it could get them some ice balls to cool them down in the sweltering June heat. The walk to the hill behind the block took half an hour. They had to meander through a sandy path past an old cemetery and a temple to the top of the hill. It was already 10.30 am and the heat was almost unbearable. The boys stopped under a tall Ficus tree and put down their things. From there, they had a bird's eye view of the whole area. The Chip Bee Estate nested just below their block which was built on the back of a steep slope. There were many *Ang Mohs* walking around down there. Some *Ang Moh* children were playing on the road outside their terrace houses.

Kai Ming had heard from his mother that these people were families of the British soldiers stationed in the country to help protect it. Kai Ming tried to match the children's looks with the descriptions of British children described in Enid Blyton's books. How accurate these were. Enid Blyton was really good at what she did.

"Kai Ming! Kai Ming! Don't dream. We have lots to do!" exclaimed Juk.

On the other side of the school was a path which led to the hawker centre. By the time the boys had reached the hawker centre, they were very thirsty and famished indeed. As they did not have much money between them, they settled for an ice ball each. It was already past lunch time and their parents would be worried sick. Though people were poor then, the family was all important and children, especially the boys were treated as small emperors.

The ice balls quenched the boys' thirst. They were pure heaven to them. But they melted all too quickly in the hot weather. In barely a few minutes the ice balls, which the boys had to use both hands to hold earlier, had been reduced to a trickle of water. Still, it had the boys lapping it all up as they trod back to their block across the road. The three boys reached their favourite spot – the landing on the fifth storey and hovered there for some time. They were hungry. Still they hated to go home. It was lonely at home. All three had no brothers to play with, only elder sisters to nag at them. It was while they were stretched out with their butts on the floor and their backs against the wall that Kirpal Singh happened to pass by. He was almost fourteen whilst the trio was only eleven even. He was also a bully and they all hated him. Standing at 1.68 metres, he was a head taller than Kai Ming, the timid one.

"What's in that bag?" Kirpal roared.

"None of your business," retorted Juk.

"This whole block is my territory and everything that happens here is my business."

"Says Who?"

"Says this fist of mine."

With that, Kirpal fisted Juk on the shoulder, catching the little boy off-guard. The surprised Malay boy landed a jab in Kirpal's groin. He couldn't hit anywhere else; he was too short. That started a free-for-all fight in which even timid Kai Ming got involved. It was three boys against one. But all that was seen was one big ball with sticky legs, arms and heads rolling on the floor.

But the boys were no match for big Kirpal who *chiak bak* most of the time. This time round, Kai Ming got the worst! A punch on his nose from Kirpal while he was grabbing hold of Kirpal's neck caused blood to ooze from his nose – non-stop. The brawl ended just as quickly as it started as Kirpal, realising the seriousness of the whole thing, ran back home. Home to him was two storeys down, in the corner flat. By now, Kai Ming's shirt had been blotted with blood and the other two boys were at a loss. It was the first time they had seen so much blood. They were frightened. Kai Ming was equally shocked and stood dazed, with his fingers smudged with blood.

Juk at last tore off to Kai Ming's flat on the fourth storey and knocked the door. Kai Ming's mother, who was in the kitchen, washed her hands and opened the door.

"Quick, Auntie. Something's happened to Kai Ming. There's blood all over him."

He brought her to the landing where Kai Ming was.

"*Aiyoh!* What have you done this time, so much blood?"

Kai Ming could not unzip his mouth. Still screaming with shock and disbelief, she took him home. The other two boys made themselves scarce. Back home, Kai Ming's mother placed Kai Ming sitting upright, with his head bent backwards to stop the blood from flowing. It took some minutes before the blood stopped oozing out. But it took all afternoon for his mother to stop her scolding. That was Kai Ming's first nosebleed. It wasn't his last. He would soon find out his nose had a propensity to bleed equal to his propensity to get into mischief when he was with his two *kakees*, Choon Huat and Juk.

After an early dinner, Kai Ming brought out his home-made *layang* and sauntered to his favourite spot on the landing. The three boys had earlier planned to rendezvous for an evening of *layang* flying downstairs in the open field. The sun had set but the concrete frame of his block still felt hot. However, a little breeze had found its way from the south to the surrounding area as there were no blocks of flats in front of his block to hinder its movement.

Kai Ming greeted his two friends who were spread on the floor with the 'glass' string laid out. Both were winding the string onto a short thick stick.

"There you are. We thought you were not coming," said Choon Huat.

"How's your nose? Did you eat *kway teow* just now? Let me look at your legs," stuttered Juk.

Juk had been worried all afternoon. He felt he had let Kai Ming down by disappearing so soon and leaving Kai Ming to answer to his mother. Kai Ming could only smile. He couldn't let out that his mother was all noise but no action, that his mother had fawned on him as he was her only son, that she would rather starve than let him starve – all things said, she wouldn't bear to cane him.

7

That night, Kai Ming couldn't sleep. It was too hot to sleep. He tossed and turned in bed, thinking about the happenings of the day – the nosebleed, the torn *layang*, everything. Finally, he got out of his bed, which was actually a foam mattress placed on the cement floor. His mother was snoring away by the window. The fan was droning away, beating the hot humid air. Big Sister's bed was empty. She was still working at the cinema and would not be back till past three o'clock.

He sidled into the living room and opened the front door. The air was cooler outside in the corridor. Loud snoring interrupted the night. It came from his neighbour's flat. Mr Samy was sleeping on the floor in the living room. The flat's front door was open but there was no grille gate. Anyone could just walk in unannounced. But nobody did when Mr Samy was around. Kai Ming didn't know why. Perhaps, it was Mr Samy's size that put thieves off. He was over-towering and his waist could fit in three Kirpal Singhs. Mr Samy was a driving instructor by day but sometimes doubled up as a bouncer at a night club along Serangoon Road. But, tonight, he wasn't at work. Kai Ming liked Mr Samy. Perhaps it was because Mr Samy had a television set in his living room and every now and then Kai Ming would invite himself into the flat to watch television. He didn't mind what programmes were showing. In fact, most of the time, only Tamil programmes appeared on Mr Samy's television screen.

Kai Ming was happy just to be able to watch television. There were few television sets in the country at the time. A television set was a luxury few could afford. The television sets then only showed black and white programmes. Colour television had not quite found its way into Singapore yet.

People who were fortunate to have neighbours with television sets often crowded themselves into the rooms where the television sets were. Many children who were not privileged to have such neighbours had to content themselves with just listening to the sounds emitted by the television sets in nearby flats on other floors. These children were huddled together in the corridor, below the window just outside such flats with television sets. They had their ears pressed to the wall. But it was common practice then and no one felt out of place. The children outside had their bit of entertainment, albeit incomplete, and the occupants of these flats with television sets, knowing perfectly well there were people outside in the corridor, relished the pride of having owned such a luxury.

Kai Ming liked Mr Samy for another reason. Mr Samy often took him out in his car, a Morris with signal lights on both flanks which flapped up to indicate left or right turns which Mr Samy was making. Kai Ming had on occasions also accompanied Mr Samy's family when they went to the temple to observe Thaipusam and other Indian religious festivals. Kai Ming liked these occasions for their riot of colours and the strange practice of sticking needles into body flesh.

"Kai Ming, what are you doing out there?

"It's already one o'clock. Why aren't you sleeping?"

It was his mother again. She had awakened to answer nature's call and found his bed empty. Reluctantly, he turned in for the night.

The story, Primary Blues, is set in the early seventies in Singapore.

Primary Blues

The June holidays soon came to an end. The rest of the year got swallowed up all too quickly and Kai Ming was now in Primary Six, his final year in New Town Primary School.

Today was 20th January 1970, the year of the Dog was just a week away and Kai Ming was barely a month into his new class, 6B. He had been made a class monitor and life was more hectic than usual. Mr Ong, his form teacher, had in recognition of his abilities entrusted him with more duties which Kai Ming could not refuse to accept. Mr Ong had treated him quite well the past year.

Today, Primary 1B was without a teacher, and Mr Ong had asked Kai Ming to keep the class orderly for the next two periods. Nervous and hesitant, Kai Ming picked up his wooden ruler and walked down the stairs to the ground floor. After a right turn, he reached the classroom. He had not stepped into a Primary One classroom in the last five years and could not visualise what it was like inside. There was incessant chatter emanating from the classroom. Holding his head up, he flapped open the French doors and marched into the class. The noise was deafening. There were little boys and girls clambering over mini-chairs and mini-desks. One or two were crying. Nobody took notice of this pretentious Primary Six boy standing in front of the blackboard. He was overwhelmed by the unexpected scene.

At last, Kai Ming recovered from his initial shock and smacked his ruler on the teacher's table, in the same manner which he had seen his teachers do. The sudden sound made all stop dead in their tracks. There was silence at last. He had been noticed at last. Heaving a sigh of relief, Kai Ming proceeded to tell the class what he wanted from them. He landed his ruler twice during his speech as if to emphasise his points. He paced up and down the classroom, taking in the curious looks of these little kids. It took some five minutes for them to size him up and the chattering resumed. First, low pitch mutterings. Then high pitch screams and shouts. The children were now oblivious to his presence. He had lost their attention.

Being the youngest child in his family, Kai Ming could, in no way, be prepared to deal with younger siblings if any, let alone total strangers. More smacks of the ruler on the table could not yield any results. He tried to hide his embarrassment but in vain. The classroom was a hive of activity. Soon, some children were using him as a carousel centrepiece. They were going around him in circles. One of them tugged at his shorts, nearly pulling them down.

Suddenly, the class became quiet. Every boy and girl froze. At the door stood bespectacled Miss Woon – Maths and Science teacher and every pupil's nightmare. Miss Pinch Fingers was what they nicknamed her. She would ask an unsuspecting pupil to come up next to her and then she would use her right thumb and index finger to pinch the unfortunate pupil's flesh. She would twist the flesh as if she was winding an alarm clock. Nobody fooled around with Miss Woon.

"If I hear just one more sound out of this room, I will make sure no one gets to go home today."

"And you, Kai Ming, don't you even know how to handle a bunch of little kids? Shame on you."

"I...I..," came the familiar reply.

Miss Woon left the room to go next door to 1C for her lesson. Kai Ming was left in the room, his mouth still sputtering out a reply to her question. Miss Woon was already out of earshot. For the rest of that period in 1B, he kept a red face and the children kept their silence. He was glad when the bell finally rang for recess. The children charged out of the classroom leaving him to his thoughts.

"Am I that useless?"

"What if Miss Woon complains to Mr Ong?"

He could get no answers to his questions. Feeling dejected, he made his way through the long passageway past the lavatories to the canteen at the other end. There were waves of blue and white crowded around the stalls. Kai Ming didn't like to push through the crowd for his food so he queued up for the free milk in the centre of the canteen, next to the assembly hall. Apparently, the authorities were concerned that many children in Singapore were undernourished and had recently set up free milk kiosks in every school in the country. This was Kai Ming's favourite drink and he could save the fifteen cents in his pocket again. When he had finished his drink, he went into the open space next to the canteen to look for his pals. Juk and Choon Huat were sitting by the drain next to the field. He squeezed between the two of them.

"How was 1B?" asked Juk.

"Oh, Those small fry," Kai Ming muttered, trying to keep a straight face.

"Well, piece of cake. No problem at all."

"*Aiyah!* Don't pretend. Your silly face has betrayed you again," quipped Choon Huat.

"Just like you to be a weakling."

"I...I.."

"There's only ten minutes left, let's play 'hum-tum bola'," said Juk, as usual, coming to Kai Ming's rescue.

The three boys, together with classmates Chen Little and Muthu, made for the field. Kai Ming was glad he didn't have to go down to 1B again that day. A relief teacher had arrived to take care of the class.

Back in 6B, poor Kai Ming became the laughing stock of his class because somehow the whole class had got wind of what had happened at 1B. Alicia and Joon Lee, the two girls sitting in front of him, were in stitches. Kai Ming felt down in the dumps. Joon Lee was his secret love and it pained him greatly to see her laughing at him. Joon Lee had been a great influence on Kai Ming. It was she who first introduced him to reading story books. He only started the reading habit to get into her good books and inadvertently got hooked into the habit. Because of this, his English Language skills had improved dramatically over the last two years. It was also she who had put some lift into his otherwise dull daily routine. He would wait for her outside her flat at Block 95 dutifully every school day and both of them would walk to school together. This was in spite of the fact they were not exactly neighbours; he was staying two roads away from her. They would perch themselves on their bags on the staircase landing beside the school's foyer, taking turns to read aloud Enid Blyton books to each other.

Kai Ming was not aware the other girl in front of him, Alicia, had a crush on him. Both Alicia and Joon Lee were very bright girls, having dominated the first three positions in class the last two years. Kai Ming could not have a better selection than either of these two. In fact, in Alicia's entry in Kai Ming's autograph book, she had penned the words:

"Sail to the east,

"Sail to the west.

"Sail to the girlfriend you like best."

Either Kai Ming had not noticed the hint behind the words or he pretended to be ignorant.

Kai Ming did not reciprocate Alicia's feelings. Perhaps, he was blinded by his love for Joon Lee. But then he was too young for such mushy things, for the three of them were only twelve years old.

After school that afternoon, Kai Ming and Joon Lee walked back to Joon Lee's block at Commonwealth Close. She lived on the ground floor in a two-room flat with her father and mother and an elder brother.

"See you tomorrow."

"Bye-bye. See you tomorrow," was the rejoinder from Joon Lee.

Kai Ming walked down Commonwealth Drive, crossed over to the Queenstown Lutheran Church and entered the front gate. He always cut across the church, to the hawker centre and thence to his block.

But this time, he was down on his luck. While treading across the basketball court, he was hit in his right leg by a stone thrown by a secondary school boy in a moment of mischief. The skin below his knee opened up like a submarine hatch. But there was no blood. Kai Ming stood speechless. He was too dazed for words or pain. He could only stare at the hole – the size of a five-cent coin. Kai Ming summoned enough courage to look into the deep hole, expecting to see a bone or two but in vain. The boy who was responsible for his predicament ran up to him and apologised profusely. This boy asked Kai Ming where he lived and helped him back to his flat. Luckily, Kai Ming's mother was not home or she would have given Kai Ming plenty to think about. The boy dressed Kai Ming's wound and left the flat. Kai Ming did not have the presence of mind to ask the boy's name.

Anyway, the wound healed in time for the Chinese New Year celebrations.

Chinese New Year's eve came too quickly. School that day lasted only two hours in the morning. Kai Ming's mother was busy preparing the altar for the prayers when Kai Ming entered the flat. There were chicken, pork, fish, duck and a host of other goodies laid out on the table in front of the altar. Kai Ming had not seen such a spread in the past twelve months.

"Keep your fingers off the chicken."

"Help me to put the bowls of rice on the table."

"Now, go wash your hands and change."

In the evening, Mother and son sat at the dinner table. Big Sister could not be back for the reunion dinner. She had to work till past three o'clock again. Reunion dinner was actually a time for the whole family to gather together. But for Kai Ming's family, it was quite different. Kai Ming could remember only one occasion in the past when his father had been home to celebrate the new year. That was five years back. The ship his father was working on happened to be in port then en-route to Amsterdam and his father had three days off. Since then he had seen his father less than four times.

In fact, Kai Ming's father had become a stranger to him. Kai Ming soon realised that he only longed for his father because his father would buy him his favourite Enid Blyton books when he was in town. It was sad actually, for the pair had drifted apart over the years and their relationship was never to improve in the coming years.

This year, reunion dinner was a quiet occasion again, not unlike the previous year. The soup was piping hot, the way Kai Ming liked it. He had no complaints that evening. His mother had made delicious and delectable food. But he was lonely.

After dinner, Kai Ming helped his mother to put money into *Ang Pow* packets. Each packet contained one dollar and ten cents. Quite a lot considering some other mothers only put in fifty cents in each packet at the time.

Though it was night outside, the sky was exploding in waves and waves of bright yellows and reds every few seconds, accompanied by thunderous clapping which deafened everyone's ears. It was time for the yearly ritual of letting off fire-crackers from the corridor. There was to be no let-up in the deafening noise or the streams of red smoke blanketing the whole area till the wee hours of the morning as every Chinese household in Singapore, rich or poor, let off firecrackers.

Kai Ming helped his mother to take down a bundle from the top of the cupboard in the bedroom. She unrolled the wrapping paper to reveal layers and layers of red firecrackers neatly branched together to form a long roll some ten metres in length. When unfolded, the firecrackers spiralled into a hexagonal mounting. She tied the mounting to one end of a long bamboo pole and carried the pole to the corridor with Kai Ming holding on to the trailing red firecrackers. She then tied the other end of the pole to a pillar in the corridor and took in her left hand the end of the trailing firecrackers with the fuse. The rest of the firecrackers were slung on the parapet.

"Go ahead. Light the fuse!" she shouted.

It was very noisy and she wanted to be heard.

Using a burning joss-stick, Kai Ming ignited the fuse. His mother quickly threw the trailing end over the parapet downwards. Then she pushed the rest of the firecrackers over the parapet. The end with the burning fuse almost reached the ground floor.

The firecrackers, having been lit, came alive and danced in the air. Kai Ming did not dare to look down. He only covered his ears to block out the deafening noise. He was soon to sorely miss this noise, for in the following year, the government would ban firecrackers in Singapore and he would never get to light firecrackers again for the rest of his life.

Both Mother and son slipped back into the flat for their neighbours upstairs had already lit their firecrackers and the corridor was covered in smoke and red paper. It was dangerous to be out in the corridor.

Kai Ming's mother took two *Ang Pow* packets out of her cupboard and presented them to him.

"Kai Ming. This *Ang Pow* is from your father. And this one is from me."

"May you have a good year ahead and pass the PSLE with flying colours."

"Kong Hee Huat Chye, Mother."

That night, Kai Ming went to bed with the red packets under his pillow.

"Wonder how much is inside this time," he murmured to himself.

Last Chinese New Year, his mother had given him six dollars in each red packet. That was quite a large sum to him. Soon, he was lost in dreamland. The thunderous clapping outside was far from his mind.

It was seven o'clock when Kai Ming opened his eyes. The bedroom light was still switched on although sunlight was glaring through the open window. It was the family tradition to switch on all the lights in the flat on the eve of Chinese New Year and leave them on overnight. His mother had said this was to welcome the new year. His mother's bed was empty and Big Sister was slumped in her bed. Kai Ming got out of bed and headed for the toilet.

"Kong Hee Huat Chye, Mother."

"Oh! You are up already. Go take a bath and change into your new clothes. Breakfast is ready."

"Remember, don't disturb your sister."

After his bath, Kai Ming slipped into his new clothes and greased his hair with Brylcreem, taking great pains to ensure his 'curry puff' hairstyle was just right. Then he had his breakfast – fried rice and chicken.

After breakfast, he went into the living room and started his wait for visitors. It was to be a long wait in vain. No one would step into the flat that first day of the Chinese New Year. He didn't realise it at first. As the wait dragged on, his mind would recall the past few new years and he would be reminded of the stark truth.

There he was, all decked out in his new year clothes but there was no one to show them to. There was also no *Ang Pow* to be collected.

Kai Ming was too young to know that as his family was poor, his relatives would give his flat a miss in their traditional new year visits. They would keep away all new year and the rest of the year too. His relatives were mostly rich people who could not get themselves to rub shoulders with the poor. They were afraid Kai Ming's mother would borrow money from them. Strangely, when people had money, they started to harbour all sorts of illusions in their minds. Only his father's third cousin, Uncle Chiam, who worked as a civil servant, could find time to visit his family from time to time.

He paced up and down the flat, taking turns to sit in the cane chair, his bed, and the stool in the balcony while drinking his favourite F&N Orange Crush. His mother noticed his impatience.

"After lunch, I will take you to Auntie Seok's place," she promised.

Auntie Seok was not even a relative. She was the daughter of his mother's friend. They lived in Tiong Bahru. His mother had a lot of friends everywhere – not those fair weather ones but real ones who would share all the joys and worries. These people more than made up for the lack of friendship from her relatives.

Big Sister was finally awake. She was brushing her teeth when Kai Ming came up from behind her.

"Kong Hee Huat Chye, Big Sister," he said.

"Mmmmmmm. Aaaaaaaah," was the reply.

The toothbrush was still in her mouth and her words were unintelligible. Big Sister had quite a load on her shoulders. It was she who had to quit school when she was in Secondary Two to help the family to make ends meet. Their father's salary was barely enough to keep the family going. It was an enormous sacrifice for his sister. Girls her age were still enjoying themselves in school and here she was, slapped with such a burden. Still, she had taken it all in her stride and accepted it as her fate. Kai Ming was careful never to provoke his sister. She had done so much for the family and he felt he owed her a great deal. Without her, he would not have had the chance to complete his primary school studies. Without her, he might not be able to go on to secondary school. This picture, thus painted, was by no means uncommon in newly industrialising Singapore. This was a common story among HDB folk. It was what bound the residents together – a common need for a better life. In the years to come, this common need would fade away as children grew up, parents became grandparents and the country prospered. Such common poverty was to become a thing of the past as Singaporeans benefited from its new stable and enlightened government.

"Mother, I have found a new job," Big Sister surprised both of them.

"I am to be a cashier at the Hyatt."

"Oh Good. Then you won't have to slog through the night again."

"All this night life is not doing your body any good."

"When do you start, Big Sister?"

"Next week. On the 1st February."

The family of three finally left the flat at about two o'clock. They were careful to avoid being surprised by dancing firecrackers let off by residents upstairs in the block. The surrounding open space was a sea of red. Even the drains were clogged with red paper, remnants of firecrackers set off the previous night. Every now and then exploding firecrackers made themselves heard in the neighbourhood. Occasionally, a live firecracker would dart about just next to where they were walking. There simply was no escape from these red things.

A public bus took them to a bus-stop along Tiong Bahru Road. They alighted and walked down a small road into the new HDB estate. Tiong Bahru at the start of the seventies was a mixture of recently built high-rise HDB flats and a scattering of low-rise apartments built in the fifties. Auntie

Seok lived on the eighth storey in a two-room flat in Lengkok Bahru together with her mother. She was still a spinster although there were quite a few suitors. Perhaps, she wanted to choose a husband carefully – one who would look after her mother and take her as his own. Auntie Seok worked as a telephone operator in a big Chinese firm in North Bridge Road. There was no doubt in Kai Ming's mind she could easily get married. She was tall, slender and quite beautiful. She was Kai Ming's favourite auntie, not only because she gave four dollars in her *Ang Pow* to him, but also because she was always around to help his mother in her hour of need.

Soon, the three of them reached her block. At both ends of the block stood two make-shift gaming stalls. Some people – still in their new year attire – were busy placing their bets. A man standing behind each stall was shuffling a deck of cards and at the same time exhorting passers-by to join the game. The lift – located up a flight of stairs in the middle of the block – took the threesome up to the landing between the eighth and ninth storeys. They walked down some steps, made a right turn and reached Auntie Seok's flat.

"Ah! Good. She's in," His mother said.

In those days, a telephone was a luxury. Out of ten blocks, perhaps you could find two flats with a telephone. Auntie Seok too didn't have a telephone so there was no way to inform her in advance of their visit. Kai Ming's mother at times would hazard a visit to her only to find the place in darkness and no one in.

An elderly woman opened the door and let them into the flat. There wasn't any grille gate at the front door.

"Kong Hee Huat Chye," wished the two children.

"Ah. You are all here. Ah Seok! Ah Seok! Look who's here," called Auntie Seok's mother.

"Kong Hee Huat Chye, Ah Mai," wished the two again.

'Ah Mai' in Hainanese meant auntie.

Auntie Seok was very polite. She was also conversant in English and spoke to Kai Ming and his sister in English. Of course, at the time, Mandarin was hardly in use and dialect was dominant in conversations. But this time round the three chatted in English. Kai Ming's mother and Auntie Seok's mother were firing off Hainanese in rapid succession. Kai Ming didn't know what they were talking about most of the time. He seldom spoke Hainanese at home. He spoke English to his sister. He never spoke Hainanese elsewhere. In fact, he was a strange sort of Singaporean for he was beginning to think and even dream in English. Perhaps, it was the influence of those Enid Blyton books. Maybe it was because he seldom spoke to others, even his own mother and so developed this deficiency.

Auntie Seok put an *Ang Pow* packet in his shirt pocket while he was busy with his F&N Orange Crush.

"May you grow up to be an outstanding young man."

"Thank you, Ah Mai."

Back home that evening, Kai Ming took out his three red packets and counted the money.

"Wow! Sixteen dollars." It was a princely sum to a young child at that time.

Auntie Seok had given him four dollars. That's worth the money in four red packets.

It was time to play with firecrackers again. Kai Ming brought out some ten-centimetre tall rockets and leaned them against the parapet in the corridor. Next, he positioned one through an opening in the parapet, took aim and ignited the fuse with a burning joss-stick. The rocket shot off in a trajectory with a loud whizzing sound. It soon found its mark in the front door of a flat in the opposite block.

"Bam!"

Kai Ming hid his face behind the parapet. An occupant of the targeted flat came out for a look. He went back in and closed the door behind him. Kai Ming launched the remaining five rockets into the sky. Then he went in search of his two pals. He had no luck on the ninth storey. Choon Huat was still out visiting. Juk, who lived on the fifth storey, came out to join him. Both boys went to the Indian stall in the hawker centre to purchase fireworks. They soon found a spot on the kerb at the corner of their block and spent the rest of the evening letting off different types of fireworks; there were fireworks shaped like motorcycles, tanks, cars and lorries. When ignited some would move off in a straight line; others would go round in circles and release a trail of colourful bright sparks.

How the two boys enjoyed that evening! Their children would never get to see such dazzling toys, let alone fire them. It was a treat that would remain etched in the boys' minds for a long time to come.

With the passing of the lunar new year, the rest of the year took a more serious note. The PSLE examination seemed to loom closer and closer. Finally, before Kai Ming knew it, he had sat for all the PSLE papers. It was already the middle of October. The year of the dog only had three months left in its run. Unknown to Kai Ming, his future wife would be born on the first day of the next Chinese New Year – the Year of the Pig.

Having to say goodbye to all his schoolmates, teachers and the school was painful. Kai Ming had been posted to Victoria School in Jalan Besar while most of his classmates would start secondary school in the adjoining New Town Secondary School. He had made sure everyone he knew had contributed some words in his autograph book. He would soon be moving to the new Toa Payoh Estate far away and there would be little opportunity to see his pals again.

The changes were taking Kai Ming by storm and displacing his mind. It was the last day of school and Kai Ming could not keep still. He would miss Choon Huat, Juk, Joon Lee, Alicia, Mr Ong and the only school he had known in his life.

Sitting on the kerb by the side of the school building, Kai Ming opened his autograph book to the page where Mr Ong had scribbled some words:

"No man is an island by himself,
either in life or after death."

23

It was an apt reminder to Kai Ming not to daydream too much, not to keep to himself all the time, but to learn to accept those around him and live with them.

Alas! Kai Ming was too young to understand the meaning behind the words.

At last, he closed his autograph book and with that closed a chapter in his life.

The story, San Yun, is set in the nineties in Singapore.

San Yun

"I don't know; you'd better tell him."

"Mr Gee won't believe me, you know..."

"San Yun. SAN YUN. Are you talking to yourself again?" asked his mother.

San Yun came out of the toilet, and washed his hands.

"You forgot to flush the toilet again. How many times must I remind you to flush the toilet?" chanted his mother.

"Okay. Okay. Why do you always nag over small things, Mother?"

"Well, you don't help in the housework. The least you can do for me is to get some decent grades for your exam. But look! You are always failing your exam," exclaimed his mother.

San Yun picked up his Digimon Two and piled himself onto the settee in the living room. He lived in a two-room HDB flat in Hougang with his father, mother and an elder sister. He would be eleven years old this April, but things were not going right for him nowadays. His mother had promised to buy him a Digimon Five, an electronic toy which responded to him much like a real-life pet, except he couldn't cuddle it in his arms. He didn't stand a good chance of getting it from his mother, though. His first term results were just in, and although he had managed to hide the marked test papers here and there, his mother, who somehow had the knack for finding lost things, had at last found his test papers.

What an unlucky week for him! It had been three whole days since that discovery, and his mother's nagging had not abated. He had lied to her about the test papers not being released by his teachers. But his mother had seen through his lie almost effortlessly. He groaned as he continued feeding his favourite electronic pet monster. How he wished exams were abolished!

Alas, it was only wishful thinking. That would never come about, even if the world came to an end suddenly. The phone rang. San Yun dragged himself out of the settee and picked up the receiver. It was his sister, Wei Ting, on the other end.

"Come down now. Jingshun is here with me. We are going over to Hougang Mall."

San Yun replaced the receiver, put his wallet into a pocket and stole out of the flat, leaving his mother still talking at the top of her voice in the kitchen. But, she had no listener now. San Yun lived on the thirteenth storey of his block, just next to the lift lobby. But, he would always walk down the stairs all the way to the ground floor. Not because he felt he needed the exercise, even if he did look as if he could do with plenty of it. At 45 kg, he was by any standard, much too heavy for his age. His belly bulged out so much that when he answered nature's call his urine would spray all over the squatting pan as he could not see what he was doing.

The truth was, San Yun was afraid to go into the lift. It was the fear of a blackout in the lift when he was inside that put him off using these contraptions. He had such a nasty experience some months ago and since then, the only times he allowed himself into the lift were when he had company.

If he wasn't in a rush, he would wait patiently till someone else found a need to use the lift and then he would quickly file into that little cubicle, albeit apprehensively. Today, he was in a hurry. He panted heavily as he made his way down thirteen flights of stairs to the ground floor. He made a few stops along the way, to catch his breath. At last, he reached the ground floor. Big Sister showed him her familiar glare. He needed no words from her to tell him she was almost through waiting for him.

"You mean he walked all the way down from the thirteenth storey!" exclaimed Jingshun.

"*Aiyah*, he's always like that, afraid of everything," replied Big Sister.

Big Sister was a head taller than San Yun. She had barely scraped through her PSLE examinations last year and had been posted to Serangoon Garden Technical School the first term of 1998 to study in the normal academic stream. Jingshun had more grey matter and that was why he could get into the express stream at Montfort Secondary School, situated a stone's throw away from where they lived.

The three of them were pals and related by blood. Jingshun was their maternal cousin. His parents had separated and he was now living with his mother. But, he wasn't happy at home. His mother had a male friend who was staying at their home in the block behind San Yun's. Because of this, Jingshun found every opportunity to get away from his home. The man did not have a job and was home all day. Jingshun couldn't stand the sight of this freeloader and had, on many occasions, fallen out with his mother over the man.

The threesome kept a leisurely pace as they crossed the main road separating their neighbourhood from the town centre. Hougang Mall stood in the background ahead. It would be a few years before Orchard Road fever bit and enthralled them. Until then, they were satisfied with just hanging around Hougang Mall. It had everything they ever wanted in its six storeys of shopping – supermarket, library,

Popular Bookstore, electronic game shops, Neoprint machines, the works!

The children made the electronic game shop their first stop. Sanyun could not keep his eyes off the new transparent Digimon Five model that beckoned to him from the glass case to the left of the shop's entrance. That little thing cost a hefty $39.95 and there was no way he could save enough money from his daily allowance to buy it, not in a million years. His entire pocket-money was spent investing in his big belly just to keep its shape at status quo. Sure, he could save forty-five cents a day if he walked home from his school. But the sacrifice would be enormous as Parry Primary School was kilometres away from home. San Yun worked out the figures in his head. He would have to walk home about eighty-eight times over the next four months just to come up with this amount. By then, his dream Digimon Five would have become obsolete! He gasped and shook his head. Big Sister, who was beside him, pressed the nape of his head with the palm of a hand.

"Wishful thinking, Little Brother."

"There's no way you're going to land your hands on that Digimon."

That day, the threesome could only browse around. Between them, they only had four dollars – good for three drinks at McDonald's with spare change left over. And that was just what they did with the money afterwards. Today was Sunday and McDonald's was crowded with youngsters and families. Every seat was occupied. The three of them ordered their drinks to go. They were glad they made this choice. It was almost noon when they left the cool comfort of the shopping centre. But, as they trod back home, drawing ice-cold Coke into their mouths, they felt really cool inside their skin although the heat from the sun was searing. When San Yun and his sister entered their flat, they found six dollars on the dining table. They understood at once that they would have to get their lunch from the coffeeshop downstairs.

Mother wasn't around. The whiff of perfume in the air told them she had gone to town and would not be back until evening. San Yun had until two o'clock to finish his lunch for his tuition teacher would be arriving then. He liked this new teacher, his third in a year. The previous two had given up on him after only one or two lessons. This one, so far, had lasted three whole months. He addressed this teacher as 'Teacher' not Mr Tan which was the teacher's last name. Teacher was thirty-something but San Yun never felt there was any generation gap between the two of them. Teacher, for one thing, never scolded him. Teacher also never set his hands on him even when he was naughty.

Somewhere along the line, San Yun understood that Teacher genuinely wanted him to try his best, not for Teacher's sake, but his own. San Yun allowed himself to go as far as feeling guilty for not doing his bit in his last exam. Teacher had said it was all right to fail this time, and that San Yun would grow out of his indifference. Teacher hoped this would happen pretty soon, for San Yun was now in Primary Five and only had another year left to repair whatever damage was done over the past few years. To be fair, San Yun was now beginning to try to put in more effort. To be honest, it would take a lot more effort for San Yun to kickstart himself. He was now showing interest in his schoolwork. Teacher had noticed the slight change in his character. For one thing, San Yun was now able to last one and a half hours in the tuition lesson without going to wash his hands. During the initial lessons, San Yun had this habit of excusing himself at least ten times during each lesson to wash his hands. San Yun was now also attentive. His face would beam each time he got a Maths sum correct. Teacher could feel an air of confidence in San Yun. Is it possible for San Yun to turn his marks around during the next few months? San Yun's face and mannerisms these few lessons showed promise.

Mr Tan was a full-time tutor. He had seventeen students under his care, most of whom lived in Hougang. All seventeen, boy or girl, had come to like this slim soft-spoken man who never got angry with any of them no matter what they did. Mr Tan would peer at them from behind his spectacles and play out his favourite phrase:

"Of course, you may .....(do something Mr Tan didn't quite like) .... in your dreams!"

That remark would send everyone into stitches. San Yun was no exception. In fact, he had rehatched this phrase on unsuspecting schoolmates several times with good effect. Today, Mr Tan caught San Yun using a clichéd expression when San Yun was relating an incident which happened in class earlier that morning.

"*Heng-ah*! Mr Samy didn't catch me bringing my Digimon to school today or he would have confiscated it."

"Are you Mr Heng?" retorted Mr Tan.

That remark tickled San Yun's ribs. His lips widened into a grin.

"Uncle San Yun," Mr Tan began.

"Have you ever forced me to do things I don't like?"

"No."

"Have I ever forced you to do things you don't like?"

"No."

"Good. We know there is no point forcing anyone to do things against his will. It may work once or twice. But it doesn't work forever."

"Yah."

"Are you Mr Yah?

"No." (chuckles)

"Good, I will wait for you to wake up from your dreams. I know a Primary Four pupil who used to fail her exams every year without fail. Till Primary Five, that is. Suddenly she changed for the better and from then on, she never failed an examination."

"Teacher, is she your student?"

"No. She's my wife. It was she who recounted her primary school days to me when I confided in her your problem."

"So, the thing to learn from this is, people do change. There comes a time when we decide to hit back at those people talking behind our backs about our grades. I hope this year is that time for you, Uncle San Yun."

There was silence in the kitchen where the lesson was taking place. San Yun's legs stopped giving the football under the table another whirl.

"Uncle San Yun."

"Yes?"

"Did you hear what I just said?"

"Yes, Teacher."

With that reply, the lesson continued. With the message digested, the football resumed its whirl. Progress in San Yun's grades was slow but noticeable. His marks inched up in the Semester Examinations. Now, he only needed six or seven marks to be rid of that disgusting red mark set against his English, Maths and Science papers. He never had a problem with Chinese, though the marks were not exactly high.

San Yun was now battling himself. He had no external enemies. It was his laziness he had to fight. It was his indifference that he had to conquer. It wasn't easy for him. This was his first try at ridding himself of a bad habit. But, he didn't want his mother to continue to nag at him. He didn't want his school teachers to ridicule him in front of the class again. Most of all, he didn't want his tuition teacher to be sad again. Not all tutors were bad after all. San Yun was lucky this time round. He had found a tutor who was genuinely concerned about him and took the pains to change him.

This change in San Yun did not go unnoticed at school. His teachers found him most willing to raise his hands to answer questions either verbally or by writing on the blackboard. One July morning, San Yun was called to the principal's office. He shuddered at the thought of seeing Mr Wong. By now, San Yun was a regular visitor. Each time he left the office, he would flap both arms downwards behind him, one red palm nursing the other and he would purse his lips as if breaking into a cry. But the cry never got out. San Yun would never allow himself to show he was fallible.

"What could I have done wrong this time? " he thought to himself.

He had no inkling why the principal had sent for him. Nervous and hesitant, he entered the principal's office after getting a reply to his knock on the door. San Yun's hands grabbed the flanks of his dark blue shorts. He tilted his head downwards, and could not see the principal's face.

"Good morning, sir."

" Ah, here you are, San Yun."

"Don't worry. I am not about to cane you again."

"On the contrary, I've heard from your teachers the dramatic improvement in your behaviour and studies. I just want to say this. Keep it up."

"Th..Thank you, sir."

"You may go back to your class, San Yun."

San Yun's hands stopped fidgeting. Once out of the room, he tore off to the toilet. He needed to regain his composure after this meeting. He peed into the toilet bowl. He could just about see what he was doing now. Over the past four months, he had lost six kilograms, thanks to Teacher. Mr Tan would ask San Yun to stand on the bathroom scale every lesson and would implore him to cut down on his weight. Apparently, this method had worked on San Yun.

His shorts weren't so tight nowadays. He had no problem buttoning his shirt anymore. And, in the process, he had saved about fifty dollars. San Yun beamed to himself in the mirror. He was delighted at the way things had turned out. San Yun still kept one of his bad habits – talking to himself. Somehow, he could not quite grow out of this habit, not yet anyway. He spent the next few minutes in conversation with the image in the mirror, then combed his hair and returned to the class.

Soon, it was report book season again. San Yun, who previously would delay giving it to his mother until the very last minute, this time had reason to smile. The page for Primary Five showed passes in English, Maths, and Science, finally. The passes were borderline ones. Still they were passes. It was the first time since Primary One he had passed. He was in a jubilant mood that day. He went on the rounds, telling one and all his feat. That evening, when he placed the opened report book on his mother's laps, she managed a smile. First a little one, which then widened considerably and in so doing betrayed the wrinkles on her face. But, she was glad the wrinkles showed this time. Not that she was glad to look old. Her only son had done an about-turn in his grades and she was the happiest woman in the world. There was hope after all. Perhaps, her son would not take after his father after all. The elder Ong had left school without completing his PSLE. He never had a stable job. It was she who took the burden of bringing up the family in her stride. It was she who slogged long hours of overtime just to make ends meet for the family and, of course, she was the one who paid San Yun's tuition fee.

There was a reason to celebrate that day. San Yun's mother took him and Wei Ting out to KFC restaurant for dinner. The family seldom went out together. As far back as he could recollect, he hardly went out with his father. His mother, too, was seldom seen together with his father outside the flat except during the Chinese New Year period when they were visiting relatives. That night, while everyone was watching television, San Yun sat at the main doorway, with his back against the door, peering out into the corridor through the grille gates. Things were not as bad for him as they were for Jingshun. Jingshun was alone. His estranged father didn't want him. His mother thought him a nuisance and an obstacle in her relationship with her live-in lover. That freeloader hated him to the core. Jingshun was left to wander outside in the neighbourhood most days.

On the other hand, San Yun had a mother who cared for him and about him. He could not have asked for more. All things considered, his life was not so bad after all. Previously, San Yun would think of his father and compare himself with him secretly. He would feel he still stood out a better person than his father. Now, his yardstick had a different measuring

35

unit. Now, he was up against his tuition teacher. He had started comparing himself with his tutor some months back, and perhaps, because of this, his life took on a new focus. He had higher expectations of himself. He had a loftier wish – he wanted to be a doctor when he grew up. He didn't want to end up like his father. He didn't want to be one of these hoi polloi.

San Yun wasn't talking to himself now. He was thinking to himself, and these were good thoughts, he admitted to himself. At last, he gave a sigh and turned his eyes to the television set. His favourite programme, Phua Chu Kang, was showing. He had missed the opening.

The story, His Father's Son, is set in the late eighties and early nineties in Singapore.

His Father's Son

The casket rolled on the conveyor belt into the furnace. Cries broke out in the hall as Pei Wen sobbed in his thoughts. He could not allow his tears to show. He was a man after all though he was only sixteen years old. As he knelt next to his mother, he could feel the anger and frustration in her cries. Aunt Caroline was by Mother's side, holding his mother in her bosom and crying above his mother's head. Several metres away, bereaved relatives of another dead man lined up in front of his coffin, ready for the cremation ceremony. But Pei Wen's mind was already far away.

He was thinking hard about the past few weeks. Things had been moving all too quickly for him and his family. His father was alive just last week. He had taken his own life exactly four days ago, on a Thursday when his mother was at the bank, sorting out her accounts with the bank manager. She was the first to find his body, slumped in the toilet bath on the ground floor and frothing at the mouth. By the time the paramedics arrived at the house, it was already too late. His father had stopped breathing and his mother was in a daze. There was no one else in the big house to tell her what to do next. She was lost. It was later that morning that Aunt Caroline, whom his mother had contacted, and her mother stepped into the house at 98 Tampines Road.

"Yoke Kuen, Oh Yoke Kuen," Aunt Caroline spluttered.

"Oh Yoke Kuen, I'm so terribly sorry to hear the news."

That brought tears down his mother's face again. Her face was sallow enough but now her cheeks sagged as well, revealing lines of wrinkles normally kept hidden behind her makeup. She was all of forty-two, a cashier turned housewife after she married Pei Wen's father. He was a bank manager in the Private Banking Department of a large foreign bank based in New York.

"Caroline, thanks for coming, I...I...really don't know what to do," sobbed his mother.

The two of them needed no more words between them. They had been bosom friends since they were young and understood perfectly how the other had felt. The tragedy brought them even closer. Aunt Caroline was his mother's cousin. Both of them had spoken to each other on the phone the evening before when Aunt Caroline had advised his mother to close all her bank accounts immediately to avoid them being frozen by the government when his father was made a bankrupt. His father was sued successfully in court by his creditors – two stock broking companies – because he had failed to pay them for his huge contra losses in his share trading facilities with them. Thereafter, everything fell apart. As the banks came to know of the suits, they jumped into the bandwagon, cancelled his overdrafts, loans and credit cards. They, then, issued demands for his father to pay up the outstanding amounts he had incurred in his accounts with them. Their house, which was mortgaged to a bank, was to be placed on the auction block by the bank as his father had failed to pay the last few instalments. His father's employer, for whom he had slogged for seventeen years since graduation, had cast a blind eye at his predicament. His repeated pleas to his employer for financial assistance to tie him over the difficult period had failed to draw any sympathy. He had been left to fend for himself. The bank watched indifferently as his father faced lawsuit after lawsuit the past few months. It even placed a hold on his father's current account with it, requiring him to obtain its approval before withdrawing any sum of money from his own account. It was, least to say, humiliating.

Each month, for the past four months, his father had to swallow his pride as he approached his colleague and friend, the officer in charge of current accounts, to get authorisation to release funds from his current account so that he could pay the household bills. The bank had cleverly arranged for the salary to be credited into his father's current account with it and there was no other way for his father to make a withdrawal except through cashing his cheques personally at the counter. His father had tried to clear his own cheques through an account with another bank to avoid this humiliation. But, each time the cheques had been returned to him unpaid and marked 'Refer to drawer'. When his father had inquired at the bank's loan department, his colleague, Andy Tay, in charge of staff loans, had put it very clearly to him that he still had loans to pay off and the bank had to ensure sufficient funds remained in the account for the loan instalments. Hence, the hold on his current account would remain.

By the time Aunt Caroline arrived at the house, his father's body had been taken to Changi Hospital for further examination, for he had died an unnatural death. While Yoke Kuen was groaning over the loss of her spouse, Aunt Caroline had the presence of mind to call up Pei Wen's principal and it was he who came to Pei Wen's class to break the news to Pei Wen. Pei Wen had dropped everything he was doing and hurried home, his eyes clearly red with shock and disbelief. He regretted that he hadn't been close to his father. His father had always come home well after he had retired to his bedroom and the two of them seldom spoke to each other. But, suddenly, his father's death had torn a hole in his heart, a hole so big, everything in it had fallen out and there was nothing left to occupy it. It was indeed a broken heart. He cried silently as he waited for the taxi. It was strange, just when he needed these things, they were never around. His tears, unable to find their way out, wetted his heart as he sat in the taxi. It was a long journey, perhaps, the longest he had ever taken in a taxi.

The roar of thunder jolted Pei Wen out of his thoughts. The drizzle outside the hall had changed into a downpour and the rain itself was now crying as if it had lost its mother. Its cries were so loud they drowned out all the wailing in the hall. Presently, the ceremony was over. It was time to go home. The group, a mixture of relatives, his mother's close friends and ex-colleagues of his father, made their way out of the hall to the waiting chartered bus, umbrellas at the ready. His father's ex-colleagues took their leave and left the crematorium in two cars.

Pei Wen led the way up the bus. In his hands, he clenched a black and white photograph of his father. His father's remains would only be released to them in three days and they would have to make another trip to the Bright Hill Temple to inter the remains in an urn which would be laid to rest in the adjoining columbarium. The return journey was quieter. Occasionally, there was chattering in the back of the bus, but mostly, there was an uneasy silence. This bus, which was accustomed to incessant chattering from students and housewives during its weekday runs for the Singapore Bus Services, today seemed stripped of all its candour. Pei Wen had not spoken a word the whole day, but then he had always been a quiet and reserved boy, and kept his feelings pretty well hidden in his heart.

At last, the bus came to a stop outside the house. After unloading its human cargo, it left hurriedly, as if it was glad to be finally rid of the mourners. There were workmen dismantling the tent in the garden. Pei Wen was directed to a new altar in the living room where his mother took from his hands the photograph of his father and placed it ever so carefully in the centre, with the elder Lee looking at them from behind his spectacles. That photograph had been culled from his father's passport. The Lees seldom took pictures together and it was most difficult to locate a befitting photograph of his father at such short notice. So, his mother, on the advice of the undertakers, had snipped off his father's photograph from the passport and given it to the photo studio for enlargement and framing.

The living room which was unaccustomed to having so many visitors looked uncomfortably full. There were Pei Wen's maternal grandparents; his three maternal uncles, their spouses and children; Aunt Caroline and her mother; Uncle Leslie, his father's elder brother, and his wife; and a sprinkling of distant relatives from his mother's side. All of them had earlier washed their faces with water from two pails strewn with pomelo leaves and were now helping themselves to food placed on two small tables at the side of the room opening into the garden.

"When do you have to move out?" asked Uncle Leslie.

"I really have no idea, perhaps next month, perhaps next week... I really do not know."

"Yoke Kuen, have you found a place yet?"

Just then, Pei Wen's grandma interrupted the conversation. Her voice boomed across the room.

"Nothing to worry about. Nothing to lose sleep over. Both of you can stay with me. You know very well my other bedroom is vacant. It just needs a little tidying up. No worry at all."

"Thanks, Mother."

"It's all over. Just forget the past. You have got to carry on. Pei Wen is so young. You just leave the rest to me. I will arrange everything for you."

"Yoke Kuen," Uncle Leslie resumed, "If you need anything, I mean anything at all, come to me. David was my brother after all."

"It's okay. I'll manage somehow. I still have some money in the bank. Of course, I will have to get a job again, what type I just now can't figure out. I'm still in a daze as it is and it will be some days before I can get myself together again. Still, don't worry your head over us, we'll manage, somehow."

"My sister is a strong woman. She won't give up just like that. I don't see how she could marry that brother of yours. I mean, he's got no backbone at all, fancy going away just like that and leaving her and poor Pei Wen alone. He didn't spare a thought about them at all."

"Teng Joo, this is not the time for such nonsense," said his elder brother.

Teng Joo was Pei Wen's second maternal uncle. He was one who never minced his words. He never could resist jabbing others when he felt like it. Pei Wen never once liked Uncle Teng Joo. He thought this uncle of his was a show-off from whose mouth would reel nothing but uncalled for remarks and ridicule. But, this time, the jibe at his father had some substance in it. Secretly, Pei Wen wondered why his father was so cruel as to leave him and his mother so early in life. Everyone would have to go, sooner or later. Why did his father take things into his own hands instead of leaving it to heaven? Try as he might, Pei Wen could find no answers to his questions. He wondered whether his mother had harboured such doubts in her mind. But, these few days, whenever he looked into her eyes, he saw nothing. Her eyes were devoid of expressions. It was as if her soul had left the body.

On the third day after the funeral, Pei Wen accompanied his mother to the Bright Hill crematorium. They were met on arrival by Aunt Caroline, who had taken a half day off from work. Together, they filed into the same hall where his father's cremation ceremony had taken place. They took turns to pick up pieces of burnt ash which were the remains of his father and place them into a yellow urn on which was inscribed:

DAVID LEE
BORN 16th July 1952
DIED 12th February 1989

The urn was then set to rest on the third level of one of many rows of shelves in the columbarium, differentiated from all other urns by a number '1129D' which was inscribed above the photograph. The Lee house was quiet the next few days. It was an uneasy calm, the kind that came before a storm. Pei Wen's mother put on a strong front, seeing to his daily needs as before, pretending nothing had changed. But her usual cheerfulness had disappeared. When he had gone off to school, she would sit by the verandah, and stare blankly into the garden for hours. There was no one to accompany her; his grandma had to work and so had the rest of the relatives. But it was quite safe. She wouldn't do anything foolish – she couldn't or Pei Wen would be all alone.

The day of reckoning came barely a week later. Staff from the Public Trustees Department stuck a notice on their main door. It required them to move out of the house by the third day and leave all furniture intact. An official affixed a sticker bearing the seal of the department to every item of furniture. Nothing except clothing was to be removed from the house. Mrs Lee had earlier, on the advice of Aunt Caroline, moved over to her mother's flat a few pieces of furniture dear to both her husband and her. She couldn't fit any more things into the tiny bedroom and had left these in the house. She was now glad her precious things were safe.

The first night in his grandma's flat was strangely uncomfortable to Pei Wen. Though he had slept over many times before, that night was new to him. He couldn't sleep. Perhaps, it was because there was no air-conditioner in the bedroom. Perhaps, it was the unending cornucopia of noises from upstairs and downstairs and the opposite block. Perhaps, it was the loud footsteps from the staircase behind the wall where he slept. Whatever the reason, Pei Wen tossed and turned until finally at four in the morning, he fell asleep from sheer exhaustion.

The next few nights were no different from the first. Pei Wen began to miss his own bedroom at 98 Tampines Road. He missed the quiet of the old neighbourhood. It was, indeed, a good place to study in, he realised, albeit a little too late. His mother, who slept in the bed across from his, got up many times in the night to go to the kitchen, whatever for, Pei Wen did not know and he did not find out. He guessed she wanted to reminisce the past from the kitchen window and didn't want to wake her up. Perhaps, it would do her a bit of good to escape from this world for a while. He, too, was guilty of such forays in class nowadays and could not complain.

It was difficult for Pei Wen to concentrate on his lessons in class. He would find himself subconsciously looking out of the French windows into the open field. But his teachers who normally would have barked at him now left him to his daydreams. His form teacher, Mr Koh, was worried for him as he was to take his 'O' levels in four months. Mr Koh called on Mrs Lee one evening when Pei Wen was out and had a long chat with her. That night, when Pei Wen was about to sleep, his mother sat on his bed and spoke to him. She stroked his hair with a hand.

"Your father left us at the wrong time, but he had his reasons. You mustn't give up. You can't give up. He was a strong man in spite of what other people have said so you mustn't blame him for what he did. If you want to, go ahead and blame his employer. Blame his colleagues who wouldn't lend him a helping hand. Blame him for having the wrong friends, but never blame him for leaving us. Your father was a proud man. He had been one all through his life and proud people cannot be humiliated constantly. They just can't take it."

She stopped for a moment to catch her breath and then continued.

"The only bank he worked for gave him an umbrella in the form of credit facilities when the weather was fine, and yet, when a storm was brewing, this same bank snatched it back from him and left him to the mercy of the elements. It is something a proud man finds hard to swallow. It is what made your father do what he did. He didn't leave any notes for us, not even a goodbye. Perhaps, it is just as well. Your father was a man of few words. I understand how he must have felt. In fact, the very morning I was at the bank, I felt uneasy, as if lightning was to strike. That was about the only message your father sent me before his death. But, the two of us to put the past behind us. We have to go on living. You have to get on with your life, and your studies – make your father proud of you.

Pei Wen soon woke up from his self-inflicted spell and began studying for his 'O' levels in earnest. Nobody knew what drove him on these days, but everyone was unanimous in finding him a changed person. They didn't mind, though.

The Year of the Pig arrived shortly. It was his first new year without his father. His mother had started work as a clerk in a property firm to support the family. Things had got better progressively. However, emotionally, his mother still needed more time to heal her wounds. More money had come in over the next few months, mostly from his father's CPF account. His father, in his lifetime, had accrued some four hundred thousand dollars in this account. The Public Trustees were unable to get their hands on this sum of money as, under the law, CPF proceeds were detached from any claims on debtors. Though Pei Wen's father had died a bankrupt, he was able to leave a sizeable inheritance to his family, untouched by any creditor.

February 1990 saw the release of Pei Wen's GCE 'O' level results. He had scored 6 'A1s' and 1 'A2', almost a miracle, considering the turmoil he had been through the previous year. His mother was elated at the news. More good news was to be heard. Over the next few years, Pei Wen immersed himself in his studies, first at a junior college and then at the National University of Singapore. He put everything else on the shelf. He never found time for relationships with anyone. He kept pretty much to himself. Soon, he distinguished himself in economics and won first-class honours in the subject. With his academic pursuits at a close, he entered national service and spent the next two-and-a-half years sweating it out in the combat field. When he completed his tour of duty, instead of taking a break like most of his mates, he pored over the classifieds in The Straits Times every morning.

He found his first job in a local bank as a retail loans officer. Just when the managers were starting to like him, as he had shown much promise, he resigned. Within a month, he had found another job with another local bank, this time as a personal financial consultant. And he would resign again after barely three months on the job. This strange practice of his went on for a few more times. But, he never had difficulty locating a job. After all, he had impeccable credentials.

Banks were looking out for people like him. Finally, it appeared as if he had found the right job at last, for he had lasted exactly four months on this latest job, that of a personal investment officer at Tai Leong Bank, a local group with twenty odd branches in Singapore. The year was 1997, roughly eight years after his father's death. It was late May and he had been posted to Tai Leong Bank's Serangoon Garden branch at Serangoon Garden Way. As a personal investment officer, he was responsible for all credit facilities at the branch, reporting directly to the credit department at head office in Cecil Street.

He struck up a friendship with the manager of the bank across the street. They would go for lunches together. The manager could get along with this fine young man who topped his class at the university, though they had a gap of some twenty-five years between them. One afternoon, while they were having their meal at the Troika restaurant three doors from Pei Wen's branch, Pei Wen broached the subject of property investment.

"Andy, you should buy another property now. The time is ripe for a killing. Trust me, it won't be long before the market moves up again. You buy at the low end and sell high."

"I don't know. The property market has gone down quite a bit and the dust has yet to settle. It doesn't look too good now."

"Look! You know pretty well the government won't allow the property market to collapse. They have got plenty of money invested in it through their proxy representatives, the statutory boards. Trust me. I majored in economics, you know. I can foretell trends."

"But I don't have enough spare money. I am already quite committed with the condo unit I am staying in now and it is just not wise."

"Don't forget, I am a loans officer. I can help you. Remember – we are friends. I mean, what are friends for, anyway? Your account with my bank is safe. Didn't I treat your clearing cheque as good last week when you were short of funds in your account? If not for that, your cheque would have bounced and it would have been most embarrassing. Fancy a bank manager having his cheque bounced by another bank. Come on, if you are afraid of everything you will never get to do big things or earn big money."

"Let me think about this first."

With that, the conversation turned to other things. That Saturday evening, Andy invited Pei Wen to tag along to a barbecue at his friend's house in Frankel Avenue. They arranged to meet on the main road outside Frankel Avenue. Andy was punctual, as usual, arriving in his grey Toyota. He had his family with him – his wife, a plumpish sort of lady whose face you wouldn't recall if you had met her in the street without her husband; and two kids, a fifteen-year-old bespectacled chap who resembled his father a little and a twelve-year-old girl with plain looks quite like the mother.

Andy introduced them to Pei Wen who then occupied the front seat which had been intentionally left vacant for him. Together, they left for the barbecue. The house was a terrace in the middle of a sloping Frankel Avenue. Both sides of the narrow lane were packed with cars and Andy had to park at the lower end of the lane some fifty metres away. When everyone had alighted from the car, Andy made his customary checks on all the doors, including the boot, just to be on the safe side. He had always been a cautious man all his life. At the gate was a young man fanning some satay on a makeshift barbecue pit. There were three boys with him.

"Uncle," the three boys called out.

Andy waved to them and led his group into the open space in front of the hose. There was a motley group of people, some helping themselves to food on a longish table, some making casual conversation. and some seated at a stone table. A voice called out to from inside the house.

"Andy, Andy. Here you are at last."

Andy introduced Pei Wen to the host, Mr Goh, who was a renovation contractor. Pei Wen learnt later that the two of them were ex-schoolmates from St Patrick's. Mr Goh held such gatherings frequently to allow his contacts in the business to mix with one another. It was his way of promoting closer ties between people who otherwise would not have a chance to interact, for they came from different walks of life. There were painters, plumbers, electricians, carpenters, bankers, some chaps from a real estate firm and one or two architects. It was an uncomfortable fit and it showed. The painters and carpenters kept to themselves, the bankers and the architects found some common ground, however, their spouses found no problems getting along with one another. Presently, Mr Goh led Andy and Pei Wen to the group of bankers and architects and they engaged in petty conversation.

"Mr Lee, so you are a bank manager," said Mr Tan, an architect.

"No. I'm only an officer in the bank. I handle all types of loans – housing, personal, you name it, we have it."

"I hear you majored in economics at the U."

"Andy must have blabbed again. Actually, it's my main area of interest. I like to be able to foretell the future of the economy. I like to dabble around with figures, so it is a proliferation of what I like to do, nothing else."

"So young and yet so humble."

"Well, Pei Wen's like that. You see, he lost his parents in a road accident when he was young and in spite of that, he has grown up into a fine young man. I am quite envious of him. I wish my son would be like him, but fat hope, that boy will never amount to anything. He can't hold a candle to Pei Wen."

"There you go again. You are making me blush all over with those remarks."

"But, it's the truth, you know."

"Mr Lee, since you are so good in this area, can you tell us whether the property market will go up again?"

"Yes, do tell us."

"Let's see, I am sure you are all aware that the government has recently pumped five billion dollars into infrastructure works on the island."

"Yes."

"This goes to show the government is committed to boosting the local property market. They inject funds so that the construction sector would be propped up. They have a huge stake, you know, through their quasi-government investment vehicles, the statutory boards. Of course, they wouldn't want their money to go down the drain. After all, it's public money. They are accountable for it. There's been some talk in the papers about reducing the land put up for sale by tender the last few weeks. In fact, just today, the radio has reported that the national development minister has approved this measure. This is bound to rev up the property market in the months to come. Less land equals less condos and other units to compete with. Am I going too fast?"

"No. Not at all."

"Mr Lee, what you have said is very enlightening, even for an architect like me."

"I have been telling Andy now's the right time to move in – get a condo, not a landed unit – then wait for the market to move up again. Shouldn't be a long wait. But, he... he's still mulling over my suggestion."

"That sounds like a great idea."

"Why shouldn't one buy a landed unit?"

"The prices of landed units have not bottomed out yet. They are still quite expensive and an investment at this time is unwise."

"What would you figure is the waiting period for practical yields on investment?"

"I would say, two to three years on the conservative side."

"Three years only. This is worth considering. Andy, you are a fool. There's money staring at you and you are not willing to pick it up. Come on, opportunity doesn't knock twice. I am in the property field and yet I agree with Pei Wen's forecast."

"Let me think over first."

A week passed and Pei Wen had not heard from Andy. Pei Wen had been busy with a new promotion programme for selling insurance to customers. His bank had switched to selling insurance to make up for the lacklustre housing loans market. He had to make trips to and from the head office to gather material and attend briefings on the new promotion. Soon it was next Tuesday morning. Andy phoned Pei Wen.

"Can you get an application form for me? I have found a condo unit over the weekend and I have put up a deposit. I need a loan for the rest."

"Sure, no problem. See you at the Troika at twelve."

The bait had been snapped up. Pei Wen sighed. He was relieved. He had spent so much time and effort setting this trap for Andy, the one person responsible for his father's downfall. He would make this man suffer. He would make this man pay for what he did to his father – nothing less would suffice.

With the loan approved, Pei Wen was in seventh heaven. In the following weeks, he began to distance himself from Andy. He offered all kinds of excuses for not being free, everything except the truth. He managed a transfer back to the head office, to work in the credit department. He schemed to get an appointment as head of the retail loans department. Soon he was working behind this desk.

That July, the Thai Baht fell, making half the banks in the country bankrupt in the process. In the ensuing months, the Malaysian Ringgit, and the Indonesian Rupiah were hit badly. The Indonesian Rupiah at one point managed an exchange of 16000 to a United States dollar, a drop of some five hundred percentage points before stabilising at 9000 to a dollar. The Singapore dollar was not spared either. It went down to a low of 1.81 to the dollar before recovering to 1.72.

By late September, billions of dollars worth of shares had been wiped off the stock market in Singapore. Shares in property companies plummeted to their lowest in a decade. Overnight, many Blue chips were selling at below a dollar. Prices of all properties in Singapore fell. Most now had a market value of just under half their worth before the onset of the crisis a few months back.

Banks were scrambling to recall their housing loans. Many property investors were badly burnt – especially those who had second or more properties. Andy was no exception. What made things worst for him was that Pei Wen was behind the scenes making sure he had no way out. Pei Wen promptly recalled Andy's housing loan on the second property. Andy's employer, the bank, didn't make matters better for him. A thirtyish graduate in charge of staff accounts at the bank treated him the same manner he had treated Pei Wen's father many years back. Pei Wen laughed in his heart. He felt Andy was getting back what he sowed. What had happened to his own father was now happening to Andy.

Pei Wen arranged for his bank's lawyers to serve legal papers on Andy at Andy's workplace. First, the demand letters, then the lawsuit, the judgement and finally the bankruptcy petition – all in only two months flat. Andy's appeals to Pei Wen fell on deaf ears. At first, Pei Wen would promise to look into the matter. He did this as a ploy. He wanted Andy to get his hopes up. He didn't want Andy to look elsewhere for help until it was too late. His sweet-talk convinced the poor Andy, who by now had turned desperate. Andy begged Pei Wen to help him. He tried to push for a meeting, but Pei Wen had many ready excuses. He did not know where Pei Wen lived though they were friends. Pei Wen had wriggled out of telling him that detail the many times they were together. He couldn't get into Pei Wen's workplace. It was restricted to staff only. He could only speak to staff at the counter and they were of no help at all – they couldn't make decisions.

On 22nd December 1998, three days before Christmas, Pei Wen pored over the notice page in The Straits Times. Under the heading 'Bankruptcy Orders' he fingered the names, one by one, till he came to one that read:

Tay Siew Chye, Andy

26B Ah Hood Road Singapore 274023.

How he laughed! Then he cried. It was a loud wailing of sorts. But it was all right. He was alone at home. He let out his frustrations, welled up over the past eight years inside him. Sweet justice, he thought to himself. He snipped the whole portion of the paper and highlighted Andy's name in blue. He had taken leave for that day. He had a place to visit. A taxi took Pei Wen to the carpark in front of the cremation hall at Bright Hill Temple. He walked inside. The hall was filled with mourners, some in black and some in blue. They were getting ready for the cremation ceremony. He took no notice of them, made a right turn down a long corridor on both sides of which was a pond with tortoises here and there peeking out of the water. He entered the columbarium, and shuffled past the shelves till he reached the one where his father's remains were kept. He folded his hands in prayer and spoke to his father in his thoughts. He told him what he had done and placed the newspaper clipping, neatly folded, under the urn. He arranged the urn such that no one would be wise to the fact there was something under the urn. He spent a good half hour in the place.

That night, as Pei Wen sat on his bed reading a book, with the television set switched on, his attention was suddenly drawn to the TV screen where a news reporter at the scene of a crime was speaking to the viewers. The television set flashed snippets of a car in which the bodies of two children were lying side by side, neatly arranged in the back seat, and another two bodies, apparently of the parents, were in the front seats. He heard this was a case of suicide cum murder. The parents of the children had apparently smothered the children to death in the car, and then left the air-conditioner switched on.

The windows were all wound up and the carbon monoxide in the car had killed the parents eventually. The car was found by some young teenagers in a remote spot in the MacRitchie Reservoir area. The camera moved backwards to show the whole car. It was a grey Toyota. Pei Wen cried in horror. The licence plate told him it was Andy's car.

Pei Wen placed his face next to the television screen to get a closer look. Just then, the screen flashed back to the newsroom where the presenter proceeded with a grim summary of the tragedy. Pei Wen was stunned. His face changed into a gory white colour. He was now crying uncontrollably. He cried as if he had never cried before. He didn't mean for this to happen. He merely wanted that guy to be made a bankrupt. He was ever so sorry. His remorse showed in his actions. He sat by his bed staring blankly at the television set for hours.

Alas, he had gone too far. His conscience had finally surfaced from beneath all that hatred. But, it was too late for his target – the man whose only crime was being too *kiasu*.

The story, The Latchkey Kid, is set in the eighties in Singapore.

The Latchkey Kid

"rRRrrrr."

"RRRRRRRR," went the alarm clock.

Yisheng tossed in bed and then turned over to reach for the snooze button on the clock.

"*Aiyah!* It's Monday again," he mumbled to himself as he got out of bed.

Instinctively, he stretched out a hand to grab the packet of cigarettes on the bedside table. He lit a cigarette and took a deep puff. Then he coughed – it was a smoker's cough. But, then, he was too young to be having a smoker's cough. In fact, he was too young to be smoking. But, he always coughed this way in the morning. Yisheng had been smoking since Primary Six and, yes, he had a 'licence' to smoke at home, though he was only in Secondary Three this year. His mother never bothered to cane him or scold him. You could say this was indeed a strange household. Father, Mother and son often smoked together in the living room, oblivious to all of society's taboos on such behaviour.

Yisheng dragged himself out of bed – a foam mattress laid on the ceramic floor – and made for the toilet. He passed his mother's room and managed a sleepy glance. Mother was asleep on her double mattress, also on the floor. She worked as a hairdresser in a shopping centre in North Bridge Road. But, she kept strange working hours for a hairdresser. She would go to work at 2 pm every day and would not be back till past midnight. He never bothered to ask her about her work though there was a speck of suspicion in his eyes each time he walked past her bedroom and sneaked a look. She alone was responsible for keeping him at school and maintaining the home.

His father, the elder Seow, was virtually unemployed. At age 45, his old man had not kept a decent job most of his life, preferring to hang around the coffeeshops, taking care of his two pet *mata-putehs* and hopping into the neighbourhood make-shift gambling parlour in a flat two blocks away when his fingers itched for a game or two. What an enormous responsibility on his poor mother! She had to support her husband on top of paying for the household's needs.

Perhaps, that was why he never respected his father. Perhaps that was why he thought his father had no right to stop him from smoking and joining the neighbourhood gang. He was, after all, following in his father's footsteps. Yisheng's excuse was that his old man did not set a good example for him. He would use this excuse to convince himself he was doing the right thing each time he got whacked by the school vice-principal for some offence or other.

Yisheng looked at the image in the mirror as he brushed his teeth. He had been nagging his mother to get him a motorcycle for his sixteenth birthday, barely three months away in January 1989. At last, she had yielded to his demands, not least because he was an only child in the family. She couldn't give him much attention most of the time; Mother and son did not often get to see or talk with each other.

When Yisheng was at school in the morning, she would be at home, doing the house chores. And when Yisheng got home in the afternoon, she would have left for work. So, Yisheng was left pretty much to himself the whole day. When Yisheng got to bed at around midnight, she was just getting off work. The two of them only got to meet and talk on Sundays, which was her off-day.

So you could say, Yisheng was a typical example of a latchkey kid. For a 15-year-old boy, he was – you could say – independent. Nobody controlled his movements. Nobody interfered in his choice of friends and nobody knew or bothered to know the type of company he brought home each day. Except for his habit of smoking, Yisheng did not seem to have any other bad habits. He never stole – he had on various occasions, in the company of friends, been urged to join his peers in snitching a thing or two from the CD shop in town, but while his friends indulged in this game for excitement's sake, Yisheng had never once stolen a thing. He was proud of himself in this respect. Though, he was poor, and had peer pressure, he had never once yielded. He had his own set of principles, and this was one of them. Of course, joining a gang was not a bad habit, at least he thought so. His gang was made up of his schoolmates and friends in the neighbourhood. They were his 'brothers' and part of his extended family. He would confide in them his deepest problems and they would lend a willing ear.

Mother had left $5 on the dining table in the living room. That was to last him through school, lunch, and dinner that day. He had tried squeezing his mother for more, but was unsuccessful. They always spoke in Mandarin, though they were Cantonese. She always gave the same reply – she had to 'feed that irresponsible father of his' too. The negotiation for more pocket money would end in her getting all fired up and mouthing all sorts of cuss words. In the end, he would give up. Anyway, things were not too bad; he had a part-time job at McDonald's in Marina Square. They paid him $2.50 per hour and he was pretty happy with that arrangement. He also got a free lunch because the meals came with the job. That way, he could save a little.

Yisheng made his way down the stairs to the ground floor. His home was on the second storey of Block 227 in Yishun Ring Road, and school was a five-minute walk down Yishun Street 21. His bosom friend and classmate, Kelvin, would join him on the morning stroll to school. Kelvin looked too young for his age. Anyone would have thought he was in Primary Six. At 1.48 m, he was a head shorter than Yisheng whose height was 1.69 m. Everyone at school called him ET. He never once expressed displeasure over the use of this nickname, and so the name ET got stuck with him.

"Did you hear about Deborah and Kee Tong?"

"Nup. What about them?"

"It seems Deborah's mother was in the principal's office yesterday."

"They say she's got pregnant by Kee Tong."

"Oh? Hah?" Yisheng was sparing with his words. He was least interested in such affairs of the heart. Perhaps, because of his parents" sorry state of affairs, he was fearful about jumping into a relationship, less history repeated itself. He did not want to end up like his father, a good-for-nothing brat. He did not want to be branded as a good-for-nothing husband. It would be a long time before he got into a relationship, if ever he got into one. He was sure no girl would show interest in him, after all, everyone at school knew his home background. Any girl would be afraid he would turn out to be exactly like his father.

"What you say, we go to your house after school?"

"Yisheng... YISHENG! What's on your mind?"

"I...erh. Nothing, nothing at all," said Yisheng. But, his eyes gave him away. Kelvin and he had been classmates since Secondary One and Kelvin could see that Yisheng's mind was light years away.

"Oh, please don't give me that again," quipped Kelvin.

"Well, actually, I am fantasising about the scrambler my mother promised me for my birthday."

"You mean, she's really, really going to buy you one?"

"Oh, yeah, I reckon so, *lor.*"

"Wow! That's great! What have you in mind?

"Well, I don't mind a Honda, you know, the one we saw last week in the carpark where Chai Seng lives."

"I wish my mum would get one for me, but that's wishful thinking. That's the last thing she would ever do. She hates bikes, you know. Says it's dangerous."

"ET! But, you are too…too…eh, I mean…too small-sized to get on a scrambler."

"Says who?"

"For goodness' sake. Your legs can't even reach the pedal!"

"They can! And I can prove it."

"Oh, don't let's argue over this early in the morning. Leave me alone to my thoughts."

"I…Look who's coming this way."

"Argh! She again? Oh my God!"

"Yisheng. Who asks you to be so handsome; girls just can't keep away from you."

"*Alamak!* Here she comes."

"Hi ET. Hi Yisheng."

"Hi. Mei Feng." Mei Feng's their schoolmate. She was their classmate last year in Secondary Two, but this year, she's gone to a different class.

"Yisheng, are you going to Swing Singapore this December?"

"Yisheng."

"ET, ask Yisheng for me. He's not answering my question."

"Forget about him this morning. His mind's far away. Why don't you ask again, like in December? It's only October, for goodness' sake!"

"ET. Are you going to Yisheng's place today? Can I come along?"

"*Alamak!* Why don't you ask Yisheng directly? Why do you always ask me? I don't want to be involved in your husband-and-wife things."

"ET. She and I are not husband and wife, okay? Please don't say things like this, *lah*."

"Good. Now he's awake. Now, he's back in this world again."

"Hah? What are you two mumbling about?"

"Oh, you won't understand. It's men's talk. Ah! We have reached school already."

The two boys were glad to be rid of Mei Feng. Kelvin was unhappy that Mei Feng was making use of him to get close to Yisheng, and Yisheng, on the other hand, was glad to be rid of this girl with hands she could not keep to herself. She would flex her arms around him as if they were an octopus's tentacles and he wasn't at ease when she was around.

It was time for the morning assembly at Yishun Town Secondary School in Nee Soon East. The whole school assembled in the parade square in front of the carpark for the morning flag-raising ceremony. When the songs were sung and the pledge recited, the students were allowed to sit on the tarmac in the parade square. Mr Ng See Teck, the vice-principal, got onto the platform. First, he went after those who were without a tie. They had to form a queue at the office to purchase a new one. Mr Ng wouldn't accept any excuses. Today, Mr Ng seemed to be in one of his black moods. His face seemed even blacker today as he was wearing a dark-coloured long-sleeve shirt.

"Boys and Girls. Today, I have an important announcement to make. It seems that one of the girls in our school has not been on the best of behaviour. In fact, she has got involved in a Boy-Girl Relationship. I have told you guys time and again this is not the time or place to enter into a BGR. But, I guess my advice has fallen into deaf ears. This school can't accept this sort of behaviour. Yesterday, the girl's parents came to see me in the office. The girl is now pregnant. Imagine that – she's only fifteen. I hope all of you will know better than to follow in her footsteps. You are here to study, to get a good certificate, not to make love. I know I am being brunt, but I think that's the kind of language you understand. I have referred the student to the ministry's students' health service. I hope there will be no more of such cases from now on. This is not something great to be talked about so I will stop here."

"Does he know who's responsible? asked Yisheng.

"Nup. I doubt so. Deborah's scared stiff. She won't give Chai Seng away for sure. He'll end up in the Boys' Home. She's not yet sixteen, you know," whispered Kelvin.

"Simon, are you coming to Yisheng's place today?"

"Sure thing," replied Simon. He was sitting in front of Kelvin in the parade square where their class 3A1 was supposed to sit. The whole class sat in a long column from the front of the parade square all the way to the middle, in single file, according to index number order. Simon, a bespectacled tall bony chap, had been the duo's bosom friend for the last three years. Both Kelvin and Yisheng knew they could rely on Simon to come to their aid when they needed muscles in a fight. Simon was quick with his legs. He was also rough in his mannerisms.

"Pass me the Mentos, will you?"

Yisheng took a roll of Mentos from a pocket and handed it to Simon when the teachers weren't looking.

"Here comes Mrs Lee. Quick. Hide the Mentos."

A thirtyish woman walked up the column of students, marking their attendance as she moved up the column of Khakis. She peered at Kelvin from behind her spectacles.

"ET. What's that in your mouth? Open your mouth and let me take a look."

"Ahhh...There's nothing in my mouth, Mrs Lee."

"Stand up, ET." Even Mrs Lee called him by his nickname.

"Why is your mouth smelling of mint?"

"My mother says that I should take a sweet before I come to school. This way, I will not have bad breath."

"Don't be a smart aleck. Were you eating sweets just now?"

"No! If you don't believe me, ask my mother."

"What's your mother got to do with this? Hah? Hah?"

"Sit down. Don't let me catch you again."

"Thank you, Mrs Lee."

Mrs Trina Lee was the form teacher of 3A1, their class. She also taught them English. Though she was a little petty, she was the sort who could give-and-take and the students were glad to have her as their form teacher. Sometimes, she would close one eye on things which they did in class. For instance, sometimes, one of them would be caught having a Walkman in his bag when Walkmans were banned in school. Unlike the other teachers, she would not confiscate such things. She would give the boy or girl a loud scolding and left it at that. And she would replay her clichéd phrase which they loved so much – "Sit down. Don't let me catch you again."

The morning droned on. Most times, it was difficult going through the day, both for the students and the teachers in the class. 3A1, after all was a class in the Normal Academic stream. It was the usual noisy class, not dissimilar from any other NA class in Singapore. Still, the class was not as rowdy as those NA classes in boys' schools. Without girls to act as a buffer, boys' schools were much noisier. Mrs Lee had come from a neighbourhood boys' school. She had suffered at the hands of the students there and so when she finally got her transfer, she almost jumped for joy in the vice-principal's office, but remembered to keep her calm. 3A1 was loads better than the 2A2 which she had been form teacher to in her previous school. Still, she pretended to be just as strict as she was when she was in the boys' school. Mrs Trina Lee came into 3A1 at 1 pm for a period of English.

The class came to attention and greeted her. Mrs Lee hated the last period of the day. She knew these students were restless at the end of the morning session and it was difficult to make productive use of them. So, she usually did individual reading aloud during the last period of the day.

Yisheng and Kelvin, who were seated next to each other at the far back in the third row from the left of the teacher's desk, were busy trying to talk above the noise in the classroom. They did not hear what Mrs Lee was shouting about in the classroom.

"Yisheng. YISHENG."

Yisheng stood up hurriedly. He had finally heard her.

"Yisheng. Please read the first paragraph of the page."

"*Alamak!*" Yisheng fumbled in his thoughts. "Which page now?" He had not been paying attention and she had caught him just when he was at his most listless moment.

Kelvin hastily flipped the pages of the textbook for him. Both of them were sharing a textbook for the lesson today.

"Yisheng. It's page 67 today. Don't you think it's embarrassing every time I have to tell you which page to read?"

Yisheng raised his voice as he read the paragraph. He was certain the others couldn't hear him.

"Class. Class. Keep quiet while Yisheng is reading. Yisheng. Start again at the beginning of the paragraph."

"rrrRing. RRRing. RRRing."

The whole class was now like a fish market. They were all waiting to go home, for the bell for dismissal had rung. They were oblivious to what Yisheng was mumbling in the classroom. Mrs Lee sighed. It was like that every day in a Normal Academic class. It was worse in a Normal Technical class. It was her fate to be given such classes. She couldn't complain. She had just stepped out of a nightmarish experience at the other school and she was anxious to make a good impression at this one, at least for the first few months, anyway.

"Class. If you behave like this again tomorrow, you will all stay back after school." She knocked her pencil case on the table.

"Class, do you understand me?"

"Yes! Mrs Lee." The students chorused in unison.

"Okay, you may go, and please don't make so much noise as you leave the class."

The boys and girls emptied into the corridors and made their way down the stairs.

It was mayhem now, as other students had joined them. The girls were chattering away, swishing their skirts as they made their way down the stairs in waves here and there. The boys were slightly more dignified at first, preferring to let the girls go down first before rushing down, pulling and tugging one another's shoulders or bags.

As they would always do so, Yisheng, Kelvin, and Simon shuffled down the carpark to the school gate, three-abreast, hands in their pockets. It was to give themselves their very own identity. As they walked, they would exchange gossip with one another. Other schoolmates passed them and the usual greetings were exchanged. Once across the street, the threesome made a beeline for their good old *mama-shop*, a provision kiosk next to the lift lobby in the void deck of Block 210. The kiosk was a good two blocks away from the school gate and made a good gathering point as another block of flats hindered any view of the kiosk from the school.

It was the group's favourite place near their school. They liked to sit on the bench next to the kiosk, surrounded by the shoulder-high paraphernalia sold by the provision kiosk, which were hung on several racks around the bench. Here was their little private space where they could gather after school. The Indian owner of the kiosk, Mr Nair, was their friend. They could count on him giving them credit when they were low on pocket money. Of course, they would pay Mr Nair the next time they were loaded with pocket money. And Mr Nair wasn't the money-minded sort of chap. He gave them credit quite freely. Perhaps, it was because they had been giving the kiosk business since they started school at Yishun Town Secondary three years ago. Perhaps, it was because Mr Nair enjoyed having them around the kiosk. They certainly made the place lively with their anecdotes of school happenings.

Yisheng headed straight for the staircase nearest the kiosk. He reached behind a drainpipe and retrieved a packet of Marlboro which he had hidden the Friday before. In his rush to school this morning, he had forgotten to bring along the packet of cigarettes in his bedroom. He borrowed a lighter from Mr Nair and drew a deep puff. He had not smoked a single stick since he left the house this morning and found relief in the cigarette he was holding in his right hand. His pals, Kelvin and Simon, were non-smokers. Though they had been with him the past few years, they had not taken up the habit. Kelvin didn't quite like the taste when Yisheng pestered him to try a stick way back in Secondary One. Since then, Yisheng had not insisted on trying to convert him. Simon had a fierce father who would kill him if he dared hold a cigarette in his hand.

Four of their schoolmates, all girls, came by the *mama-shop* and joined them in chit-chat. All four were smokers. Margaret, Mei Chen, Jing Ying and Daisy weren't the type of girls any decent boy would want to get tangled with. For one thing, all four were not exactly dainty creatures. They came from broken homes and were street-wise. They hung out with teenage ruffians in the neighbourhood. Although Yisheng and his group were part of a neighbourhood gang, the three boys likened their own gang as a tame version compared to the unrestrained girl gang that these 'ladies' belonged to. The boys were always careful not to provoke the four girls, who were notorious for getting into fights. The boys thought that as long as they kept their distance from the girls, it was alright to engage in innocent chatting. It was getting crowded in the small area, but it was fun. The teenagers exchanged stories and laughed at each other's antics.

"That Mrs Tan – Dawn Tan you know – went into the toilet to look for trouble. She thought she had caught me smoking, you know. *Heng-ah*, I threw away the cigarette in time or else," boasted Jing Ying.

"Did she find any cigarette on you?" asked Kelvin.

"*Wah!* ET, lucky for me, it was my last stick. Otherwise, you know."

"You mean she didn't smell your fingers, hah?" Simon pitched in.

"Oh! We girls are smarter than her anytime," taking out a ballpoint as she demonstrated how she smoked in the toilet.

"You see, I clip the cigarette in the handle of the ballpoint and hold the ballpoint instead of the cigarette. That way, she can't smell anything because there's nothing for her to smell," she continued.

The small group broke into laughter. Then, they restrained themselves. One of the girls stood up and looked above the toys and foodstuff hung on the racks.

"Coast is clear. Continue," said she.

"*Aiyah*, let's talk about the Tea Dance this Saturday," Daisy, who had been quiet all this while chipped in.

"Aren't you boys going to Fire Disco this Saturday?"

"Of course, *lah*," was the reply.

"Shall we go together?"

"I think it's best we meet you girls there. You know how it is with you girls, taking so much time making up. I don't think we all want to wait and wait and wait for you, especially on a Saturday," said Simon.

The other two boys nodded their heads in agreement.

"*Wah Lau!* You are talking as if we purposely delay meeting you. OK *lah*, set *lah*," said Jing Ying to the boys who were getting ready to move off.

"Where are you chaps going?"

"To Yisheng's place."

"See you!"

"Luckily you came up with that excuse, or else we'll be stuck with these *Ah Lians* for sure," quipped Yisheng.

"Don't worry. Trust me. I know how to handle these girls," was the reply.

The boys climbed up the stairs to the second storey, turned left and filed past the corridor to the end of the block where Yisheng was staying. Yisheng grimaced as he looked at the pair of shoes on the steps in front of his flat.

"My old man's in."

As the door opened, they saw Yisheng's father squatting in front of the TV set, next to the entrance to the flat. He was fidgeting with the controls to Yisheng's Nintendo set. They saw that he was playing the game, Super Mario Brothers, on the TV screen.

"Uncle," said the two boys in unison.

"Mmhh. Ah Simon, you are here. Come, join me in the game. It's not much fun playing alone," said Mr Seow.

He was a gruff man with unkempt hair; his complexion had darkened through exposure to the sun. Mr Seow, when he wanted to work – or more accurately, when he was in the mood to work – was an odd-jobs labourer. Most of the time, he would do painting of the exteriors of buildings. That's why he was dark-complexioned. Yisheng, on the other hand, was as fair as his mother. In fact, Yisheng had once told the other two boys that he could never become dark. He had said, to the amusement of his two pals, he inherited his fair skin from his mother.

The two boys were regular guests in the house, so they needed no help at all once they were in the house. They made themselves at home immediately. Yisheng, still in his uniform, went into the kitchen to cook Maggi instant mee noodles. He opened three packets – enough for the three of them. They had not eaten since recess and were famished. As he boiled the noodles, he broke three eggs and emptied their contents into the pot of mee. Next, he added the seasoning which came in little packets with the mee. He stirred the mee and shook some pepper into it. When the mee was cooked, he dished it into three bowls, making sure the portions were equal.

It was the cheapest meal available, and he could prepare it anytime of the day or night. And it only took two minutes of cooking time. Yisheng had become quite an expert at cooking instant mee. You could say he had grown up on instant noodles. He had had countless bowls of these noodles since primary school when he was left all alone in the flat. His father, who was around in the house some of the time, never once bothered to cook for him. Neither did he buy food up to the house for him. So, Yisheng had to fend for himself all these years while Mother was away at work, which was perhaps why he never once asked his father for his opinion about anything. But, Mr Seow was his father, after all. He had to accord him with the due respect that a son should accord a father. Other than that, Yisheng felt, he did not owe his father a single thing.

As he took a bowl of mee from Yisheng, Kelvin pointed in the direction of Yisheng's father and his eyes looked enquiringly at Yisheng.

"Forget about my father," Yisheng's eyes seemed to say in reply. Yisheng had not prepared an extra bowl of mee for his father.

"Go ahead, eat it while it's hot," said Yisheng to Kelvin.

Both boys ate in silence as they watched Simon and Mr Seow jabbing their fingers at the controls in their hands. The three boys spent the afternoon taking turns to play the game. Then they switched to Street Fighter. That was how boys in the 80s spent their time – Street Fighter and the Super Mario Brothers were the craze those days. Parents would fork out some $500 for a Nintendo game set, which would come with two free game cassettes. If purchased alone, each cassette cost some $100. Yisheng's mother had bought the Nintendo set for him last year on his fourteenth birthday, after he had nagged her continually for several months, at first dropping hints here and there, and later begging for it directly when the hints were ignored. In fact, if you stop and think, you would know that it was Yisheng's mother who had given him the things he wanted. His father, as far back as Yisheng could recall, had never spent a single cent on him. But, he still had to call him Father, anyway. But, respect him? Never in his life! This whole process would go on churning in Yisheng's mind repeatedly.

Yisheng's father left the boys to themselves at about five o'clock. He said he had some business to attend to. The boys lost track of time as they immersed themselves in the game. Then the phone rang.

"ET, answer for me, will you?" said Yisheng, who was playing against Simon.

"It's Siew Ling."

"Ask her what she wants."

"She says she wants to come over to your place tonight at 8 pm."

"Tell her I won't be free."

"You tell her yourself," retorted Kelvin. Apparently, Siew Ling was angry that Yisheng would not come to the phone and had vented her anger on him.

"Just put down the phone."

"Hah? Just like that?" his eyes looked inquiringly at Yisheng. Getting no further response from him, Kelvin replaced the receiver and sat down next to him.

"You two hah husband-and-wife team should keep your squabbles to yourselves and not get others involved."

"ET. I don't want to have anything to do with her."

"But, Yisheng, you are a pair made in heaven. One so handsome and the other – *wah* – so beautiful. And you say you don't want her? You must be crazy!"

"How to want her? You know my background. I can't offer her anything. But Jarren can. His family runs a provision shop and his father has a car. He can give her a better life than me."

"Why do you look down on yourself?

"ET, I agree with Yisheng," Simon chipped in.

"If I were Yisheng, I would do the same thing. You know we come from broken homes."

"Speak for yourself," Kelvin interjected, "You may come from a broken home, but not me. My parents are loving and they take good care of me."

"*Aiyah*, you two shut up. I want to concentrate on my game and I can't do so with all this noise."

"Same here," volunteered Simon.

"You two carry on. I'm going home," said Kelvin as he slung his bag and stepped out of the flat.

"ET, why are you like that?"

"ET… Come back."

But Kelvin was already out of earshot.

"He's very petty."

"You know he's like that and you purposely add fire."

"*Aiyah!* He will be okay afterwards. He's always like this."

"I am not playing anymore. I'm bathing. Can I use your towel?"

"Sure thing. Let's bathe together. We have got to be at the coffeshop at 7 o'clock tonight."

As members of the neighbourhood Ang Soon Thong gang, it was their duty to watch the coffeeshop at Block 230, a four-storey block of flats with shop units on the ground floor. The coffeeshop was situated next to Block 228, which was a block away from where Yisheng stayed. Simon stayed two blocks away, in Block 231, in a four-room flat. Kelvin stayed farthest from the coffeeshop, his block just across the road from the school gate. The three boys were part of a ten-member group in charge of affairs at the area surrounding the coffeeshop. They were supposed to keep rival gang members out of the place. If they were to see any such people, they were supposed to call up the rest of the gang for help to throw the chaps out of the place. At least, that was how it was supposed to work anyway.

But, in practice, the boys merely sat at a round table in the five-foot-way at the far corner of the coffeeshop and engaged in chit-chat. They were gang members in name only. Schoolmates who lived in the immediate surroundings would gather at the coffeeshop after dark and they would pass the time smoking away and rambling about their exploits. There were no true gangs in Singapore in the 80s. The real gangsters had been exterminated, or put away behind bars in Changi Prison. What were left were only loose groups perpetuated by unruly teenagers from neighbourhood schools who were bent on getting a name for themselves, and this they did by tagging themselves as gangsters and going around harassing fellow students.

By virtue of their built and the size of their membership, they could more or less control other teenagers at school. But, it was pulling wool over people's eyes to describe them as gangsters. They were anything, but gangsters. These teens were delighted to belong to a gang as they could use its backing when they got into trouble with other teenagers.

David saw Yisheng and Simon sitting at their regular meeting spot at a table. He came over to say hello. David was 16 years old, a student of Naval Base Secondary School. For his age, he looked very mature. It was this look that helped him to get into pubs during the weekends. He asked the two boys to join him at American Corner that Saturday night.

"You sure we can go in?" asked Yisheng.

"Trust me. I know the bouncer. No problem at all *lah*," said David. With that statement, he headed home, to the block just behind the coffeeshop.

"Remember to come," he shouted as he moved out of sight.

"Uncle. A packet of Marboro, please," said Yisheng to the coffeeshop assistant who was cleaning the table next to theirs.

"My father took my packet of Marlboro just now," Yisheng explained.

"Where's ET? He's still not here."

"I guess he's still upset. He's always like that."

The boys called for a big plate of fried rice and shared the food. They were hungry and it was their only meal of the Chinese staple, rice, for the day. As they were tucking in the food, Tommy came up to them, drew a stool and sat down. Stretching both arms wide above his body, he managed a yawn.

"Seen Min Liang lately?"

"Nup!"

"The idiot. He owes me $10 and he's hiding from me. I can't find him anywhere."

"Who asked you to lend him the money. You know he's famous for not returning what he owes and yet you lend money to him. You deserve it, *lor.*"

"Don't say things like that, Simon. Come on. He asked me for the money in front of so many girls, I just couldn't refuse."

"Girls will be the death of you," said Yisheng.

"*Wah!* You part with your hard-earned money because of your ego, hah?" Simon just couldn't believe his ears.

"What can I do? You know I want to look good in front of these damsels. That's my character. I can't change my character, can I?

"If you two see Min Liang, tell him I am looking for him. By the way, where's ET?"

Kelvin was Tommy's cousin. Their fathers were brothers. Tommy was now in Secondary Four this year. He was in the Normal Technical stream, and this year would be his last year in school. He was also a flirt. He had had so many girlfriends the boys had lost count.

"Are you still with Diana?" asked Simon.

"Yeah. She sticks to me like glue."

"I get the impression you don't fancy her. But she treats you very well," said Yisheng, "I've never seen any girl so devoted to a boy like she's to you."

"You'll make a good pair," said Simon, "At least, she will be able to change you out of your flirtatious ways, ha ha ha."

"She's the only one who can handle you," said Yisheng gravely.

"Let's not get deeper into this. Where are the others?"

"Don't know."

"Jing Yu is here. Hi."

"Tommy! Glad to see you. Where's your other half?"

"Don't be like that *lah*. We have just met and you start teasing me."

"You see, even Jing Yu agrees with us," said Simon.

"Are you guys playing billiard on Saturday?" asked Jing Yu.

"At King's?" asked Yisheng.

"Yes. Shall we meet there?" asked Jing Yu.

"How about Sunday?" suggested Yisheng, "We have got to go to Fire Disco this Saturday."

"Ok *lah*. Can I join you on Saturday?" Jing Yu looked inquiringly at the faces around him as he spoke.

"How? Can or not?"

"Okay *lah*!" said Simon, "All five of us right?"

The four boys nodded their heads. They were sure Kelvin would tag along with them that Saturday.

Kelvin was back to his usual self the next morning at assembly. He had apparently forgotten about the little episode at Yisheng's house the day before. He pushed his face next to Yisheng's and flashed a broad smile.

"You guys going to Fire Disco or not?"

Yisheng and Simon nodded their heads. Simon was in front of Yisheng in the morning assembly and could not turn his head to look at the two, for fear of being caught by the vice-principal, who was now on the platform, giving those who had gathered for the assembly a stern look.

"Boys and girls. Today is hair-check day for the upper secondary students. Mr Lee and Mrs Tay will be checking all the Secondary Threes, Fours and Fives now. Those who are singled out are to come out here and sit next to the canteen steps, the boys on the left and the girls on the right. Mr Lee and Mrs Tay, please go ahead."

Mr Lee was the disciplinary master for the school and Mrs Tay was his assistant. She was in charge of the lower levels while he looked after the upper secondary classes. Today, she was helping to check the girls for unkempt hair and forbidden hairstyles, such as dyed hair.

The three boys tilted their heads gingerly. They did not want to be caught. Kelvin's hair was curly and he could get away with having thick hair. But, Yisheng's hair needed hair cream to help it stick together. He had forgotten to apply hair cream today and he was sure it was in a mess and he would be called out. Simon was sure he would be caught. There was totally no slope at the nape of his head where his fair fell down in a sweep. Simon quickly crawled through the two rows of students on his right and headed for the toilet. He was sure no one had noticed him. The two teachers doing their rounds of hair-checking were at other end of the assembly, where the Secondary Fives were seated. As he got to his feet, he slapped the dirt off his long khaki pants.

This time, Mr Lee, who was in a particularly good mood today, had singled out only nine students. He was busy recording down their names. Those caught had to have their hair cut properly that day and report to him for a hair-check the next day. Mrs Tay, nicknamed 'Ang Moh Tay' by successive generations of students taught by her, caught six girls. They received an earful from her before being let off with a warning to get their hair cut or tied properly.

The morning assembly was soon over, and the students snaked up the flight of stairs to their classrooms. There were councillors on duty to keep them in herd during their movement up the stairs. Some of the students jabbed playfully at the councillors as they moved along the corridor, and up the stairs. Others shrugged along; they had a full eight periods of lessons ahead. Most of them were resigned to spending the rest of the morning in the company of books. Some of them, the bookworms, seemed full of zest. It was easy to make them out – they were bespectacled, and prim and proper, the goody-two-shoes type. Somehow, they seemed out of place in this neighbourhood school. Simon appeared from out of nowhere and joined 3A1 as they clambered up the stairs.

At the top of the stairs, on the third level, the procession split into their classes. 3A1 lined up outside their classroom, the first next to the stairs on the third storey, as the other students filed past them. Mr Ee, their Mathematics teacher was standing at the head of the line. He had been waiting for them there. Their first two periods was Mathematics, a subject which most of them hated to the core.

"Move in, two by two. Don't go by the back door," ordered Mr Ee.

The students moved quietly to their seats and settled in. There was hardly a noise as they did so. It was so unlike a Normal Academic class to be so quiet. There was only one reason for this – Bulldog Ee. Everyone in the class hated Bulldog Ee. He was the National Police Cadet Corp's (NPCC) officer-in-charge. Though this was 3A1, Bulldog Ee regarded everyone in his class as a cadet and expected everyone to behave like a cadet. He was Mr No Nonsense himself. Bulldog Ee sat in his chair, took out a textbook from his big attaché case and flipped open the textbook. As he did so, he tilted his head above his wide-rim spectacles – those bifocals which allowed reading of small print and viewing far objects; you knew they were bi-focals because a line ran through the middle of the lenses horizontally – and surveyed the class. There was pin-drop silence all around.

"Now, let's turn to page 115 and try the exercise there."

Bulldog Ee didn't need to say more. It was understood that the students had to complete the sums on that page during that two periods and hand them in at the end of the lesson. So much could be inferred from just that single sentence. He had the class totally under his control, it seemed. But, to be fair, with Bulldog Ee as their Maths teacher, everyone had better grades. Yisheng, who used to get a C5 for the subject now found himself with an A2 for Maths during the mid-year examinations. It was a miracle! Somehow, Bulldog Ee had found a way to produce results in his classes. The students' only complaint was he used the fear element unsparingly. Still good results were good results – that was the undeniable truth.

The students were glad to be rid of Bulldog Ee when the bell rang to signal the start of the third lesson for the day.

"Ah! Chinese now," muttered Kelvin. He had forgotten Bulldog Ee had left the classroom.

"*Aiyah!* ET. He's long gone. You can raise your voice now," exclaimed Simon.

Kelvin blushed. By now the atmosphere in the class had changed. It was now having its market-place buzz. The girls were giggling in the back as the Chinese teacher stepped into the classroom. Mr Wu was now into his fifties. He was bespectacled and had streaks of white hair going all the way from his forehead to the back of his head. He was good-natured and carefree. The students were, by now, used to his ways and carried on their little chit-chats as the lesson was being conducted. Mr Wu never seemed to mind.

For the students, it was a relief to have Chinese period after their Maths. It was a total change for them – moving from hell back to heaven, so to speak. During Mr Wu's lesson, one or two of the boys wandered out of the back door into the corridor. They were on their routine rounds again – that of disturbing the neighbouring class, 3S4. Mr Wu ignored their little foray and carried on with his lesson as if nothing had happened. He was oblivious to such happenings; he had just three months more to go before his retirement in January next year and he wasn't going to risk getting his blood pressure up by going after these boys. Since they weren't interested, he thought he would pretend they were not in the class at all.

The bell rang for recess. Suddenly there was pandemonium in the school. The students from the upper-secondary levels poured into the corridors and made their way down the stairs. Some of them were running; some half-dashing and others striding. Yisheng and his pals, Kelvin and Simon, headed for the open corner behind the ground-floor toilets at the back of the school. It was their usual gathering point. Their other classmates and some friends from the other classes would join them later – after their meal – and all of them would sit, in single file, on the kerb next to the carpark. There, they would exchange the day's news and gossip. There were no girls in the group, however. The girls had their own hangout adjacent to the school canteen.

Yisheng had two sticks of Marlboro in his pocket. He did not bother to hide them in his underwear anymore. He used to, when he was in Secondary One, but the inconvenience bothered him and nowadays he just plain didn't bother. Yisheng longed for a smoke. He got up and entered the boy's toilet, leaving the others in their chit-chat. His close pals did not smoke and he had to enjoy this moment all by himself. Yisheng turned to the far end of the toilet, hidden from the main entrance by a storeroom which stood between the other cubicles and the end wall, providing just three by two feet of room to manoeuvre in. Just then, Darren from 2A1 appeared in front of him.

"Ah, have company today," Yisheng said in a low voice.

"You got a lighter?" asked Darren. Darren Yeo should be in Secondary Three this year, but as he had failed five subjects the previous year, he was retained in Secondary Two for another year. But, he was not bothered at all. School was a drag to him. Despite all sorts of warnings and frequent canings, he remained unchanged – he was defiant and had no interest in studies. In short, he was incorrigible. Yisheng and Darren were classmates in Secondary Two and so knew each other well. Yisheng used to visit Darren's home in Sembawang. Darren came from a well-to-do family. He lived in a semi-detached house with his parents. He was the youngest of three children – two boys and a girl. Darren's brother was in 4A1 this year in the same school. His sister was at university. Both Yisheng and Darren were avid motor-bike lovers. Sometimes, we would ramble on and on about motorcycles.

"Old man Ng is not around. His car is not in the carpark so I don't think anyone will disturb us in the toilet," said Darren. It was usual for students to exchange such information when they met. This 'coast is clear' flag was necessary for the smoking of cigarettes to continue. Anyway, one of their classmates was standing at the entrance to the toilet, ready to raise the alarm in case any teachers passed by.

"The small space could hardly hold two persons comfortably. But then, both boys were slim-built – in fact, underweight – and had no problem squeezing into it. They were careful not to spray smoke into each other's uniform.

"What are you boys doing here?" said a loud voice. The duo flicked their cigarettes out of the louvered window above them. Mr Low came into view. Mr Low was their Maths teacher in Secondary One. He was slowly balding, but managed to hide that fact through careful combing. Each time he went under the fan, he would meticulously comb his hair. The students knew about his habit of combing his hair all day long, but they were not privileged to know the reasons for his doing so. Mr Low stared at the two boys.

"There's cigarette smell all over the place. Have you been smoking?" he demanded to know.

"We...eh...eh," muttered Yisheng, wondering what had happened to the lookout.

"Why do you bother?" retorted Darren. It was his usual way of talking to everyone, including the teachers. The only persons exempt from witnessing such behaviour were the principal and vice-principal. Darren wasn't exactly afraid of them. He was just afraid of getting an earful from his parents when they got wind of the complaints.

"Come with me at once," ordered Mr Low. He was clearly angered by Darren's arrogance.

The two boys could do nothing but follow him. As he walked towards the principal's office, he would turn his head around to make sure the boys were following him. By now, many curious eyes were turned on the two boys. It was recess time, and everyone had had their fill and was looking for things to do. This episode provided these chaps with fodder for after-recess chit-chats.

The two boys were ushered into the principal's office. They were unlucky today. Mr Ng, the vice-principal, was not in school. The principal's hand at caning was more potent than Mr Ng's by at least ten times. They did not relish having their butts pared by the principal.

"I have told you time and again not to smoke. Yet, both of you have chosen, time and again, to disobey me. I have got to knock some sense into you. I am going to call your parents today and ask them to see me tomorrow morning. In the meantime, I am going to give you each three strokes of the cane," said Mr Balagopal.

"Do you have anything to say?" he continued.

The two boys had their heads bowed and their hands folded behind their backs. They knew they could not escape the cane this time.

"Now, empty your pockets onto the table."

Darren took out his things first and laid them on the table. There were his wallet, a pager, some keys and a packet of Salem. Yisheng emptied his pockets. He was reluctant to fish out the single stick of cigarette in his right pocket, but in the end he took it out and laid it onto the table, beside his wallet, keys, a packet of tissues and a roll of Mentos. The evidence of their wrongdoing was now laid bare on the table. The principal needed not go through the hassle of wrangling the truth out of them about what they were doing in the toilets.

"Don't you know you are not allowed to bring a pager to school?" he said, looking at Darren.

"Okay. Now pull out the insides of the pocket so that we know the pockets have been emptied totally."

The boys complied readily. Mr Balagopal stroke his face with fingers from his left hand, paused a moment and went on.

"Take back your things and follow me," he said as he got up from his seat and made for the general office, outside his room.

"Thank you, Mr Low."

That was Mr Low's cue to carry on with whatever he was to do next. Mr Low left the room. Mr Balagopal approached the doorway to his room, his right hand flapping two thick rattan canes against his pants. The canes were at least five feet long each.

"Come, let's go," he told the two boys.

The three of them walked up the stairs to the second level where Darren's classroom was and Mr Balagopal interrupted the teacher who was just about to begin his lesson.

"Sorry, Mr Lim. May I borrow a chair?"

Mr Balagopal took the chair and placed it in the corridor with its front facing the adjoining courtyard. He beckoned to Darren. When Darren had taken up position behind the chair, Mr Balagopal passed him a small blue book, for him to place on his back, just above his buttocks. Mr Balagopal was precise in his caning, but he felt safer having his students place this blue book on their back, just in case the cane went off its intended target.

Yisheng looked on as the caning was carried out. Mr Balagopal bent his legs at the knee and took some practice swings with one of the canes he had brought along. It was like watching a golf game; the swings Mr Balagopal made were similar to those of a golfer's Yisheng had seen them on television before. Darren by now was tense. He did not know exactly when the cane would land on him, and his fingers twitched as they held onto the chair in front. Mr Balagopal swung the cane up to about 80 degrees to the horizontal and brought it down on Darren's buttocks with such force that a loud swishing sound could be heard.

Darren's fingers let go of the chair momentarily, and just as quickly, clutched it again. It was clear he was in pain. But, he was careful not to show it. The second and the third strokes were released on Darren's buttocks, and he was allowed to return to his class. By now, curious faces could be seen poking out of the classroom doorways – some belonging to students, and others belonging to teachers. But, no one came out into the corridor.

Yisheng tagged behind the principal up the stairs to his own classroom and, as ordered, took out a chair. He adopted the usual position behind the chair as the cane was being brought down on his buttocks – three times in all. The pain was intense. He was close to tears. He knew the others in the class were watching, if not trying to hear, what was happening outside the class. He had no time to think about his classmates. He also had no time to be embarrassed. His mind was a blank, not knowing when the next stroke would land on his buttocks. When it was all over and Mr Balagopal had left, Yisheng carried the chair into the classroom and excused himself. He didn't even know which teacher he was talking to. His eyes were all red and teary. He fought to keep back the tears. All he wanted to do was to get out of the classroom and go to the toilet for a good cry.

Once inside the toilet, Yisheng splashed water all over his face. His tears, which had been welling up in his eyes, joined the running water as they poured into the long porcelain sink. It was minutes before Yisheng brought his face out of the running water. He gazed in the mirror and fingered the bulging eyebags under his eyes. Now, everyone would know he had been crying, he thought to himself. He wiped his eyes with some tissue paper, took a few more minutes to compose himself, and walked out of the toilet. It was an unsteady walk, but it was all he could manage. His buttocks were still hurting and he was feeling panicky inside. His nerves had not yet steadied themselves.

In the classroom, he carefully sat down in his chair, placing his hands beneath his buttocks on both flanks. For the rest of the day, he was completely silent and in a world of his own. Kelvin knew the best way to console his pal next to him was to leave him alone. So, apart from handing him the worksheets and then passing them back to the front of the class, he left Yisheng alone. The other teachers, who had by now heard of the matter, also left Yisheng alone. Some of them knew Yisheng to be a smoker, but had kept that knowledge sacred in their hearts as they were aware of his family background. They were unlike Mr Low who, although knowing it, chose to harp over Yisheng's bad habit and found fault with it. In Mr Low's eyes, he was merely doing the boy a good deed, for the boy's ultimate good.

It was indeed a bad day for Yisheng today. He thought that nothing worse could happen as he lugged himself up the stairs to his flat. He was alone that afternoon. His pals knew he wanted to be alone and had parted when they reached the school gates earlier. Yisheng flung his schoolbag onto the settee in the living room and turned on the hi-fi set. He played Hotel California, by the Eagles. It was his favourite song. He would play this song whenever he was in a bad mood. He didn't know why, but it made him feel at peace with himself even though it was pure noise to other people.

It was two thirty in the afternoon – time for lunch. Yisheng wasn't hungry. He had no appetite. Drawing in cigarette smoke into his lungs, Yisheng stood at the window in the kitchen. Then he tilted his head towards the mirror and looked in it. His eyes were not puffy anymore, but the redness remained. It would take a whole afternoon for it to go away, he thought to himself. Yisheng headed for the TV set in the living room, He would have a game of Street Fighter before making himself a bowl of Maggi mee, he decided.

But, his Nintendo set was not there, where it should be sitting, on the floor next to the TV cabinet. The game control devices were also missing. He searched all the rooms in the flat, but in vain. Then he realised what had to be the truth. His father had taken it. His father had, most likely, sold it for money. The elder Seow had been known to take things from the house to sell when he was down and out, in dire need of money, and nothing in the house was safe from this chap. He remembered a recent incident in which his old man had ripped open a drawer in his mother's room to get at some cash. His mother had a violent quarrel with his father following that incident and since then they had not spoken to each other. That was some five months ago!

Yisheng's heart sank. His beloved Nintendo set was gone now. He knew that he would never see it again. He hated his father. He hated him to the core, not only for taking away his favourite possession, but also for messing up his home. That good-for-nothing idiot, he scolded his father in his thoughts. It clearly wasn't his day that day. His lousy mood was sure to stick for the rest of the day. Yisheng went through the afternoon without his lunch. Most of the time, he was doing nothing, just staring blankly at the place where the Nintendo set used to lie. He did not answer any calls. Kelvin tried calling him a few times, and waited till six o'clock before hopping over for a visit. Kelvin was sure the boy's mood would have changed for the better by then. Being together for the last few years, the two boys could sort of predict accurately their pal's behaviour.

"Yisheng. Yisheng!" cried Kelvin. He had knocked at the door but there was no response. Yisheng, I know you are in there. Open up."

Yisheng opened the front door and handed Kelvin some keys. Kelvin let himself into the flat.

"Why is your face still like Pao Kong's?" asked Kelvin. (Pao Kong, a judge in the Song Dynasty, is a legendary figure. He had a black face.)

"Look!" Yisheng stammered, pointing at the floor next to the TV set, "It's gone! My father has sold it."

Kelvin understood immediately what had happened. Both boys leaned against the wall adjacent to the TV set and stared at the opposite wall. Kelvin could do nothing but wait for Yisheng's mood to change. He knew Yisheng would not go out that evening, so he got up and walked into the kitchen. There, he made some Maggi mee for the two of them. He was accustomed to helping himself at Yisheng's home and did what he wanted automatically – there was no need to ask Yisheng for permission at all.

"Come, let's eat."

They left the TV set on for the rest of the evening though they were not watching. They just wanted to have some sounds in the living room, as neither of them was talking. Yisheng's father did not return that night. The two boys waited till midnight, and Kelvin went home. He had to rise early for school for next day. Yisheng would have to wait alone for his mother to return from work.

"You coming to school tomorrow?"

"Don't know."

"Wait for you as usual?"

"Okay, *lah*."

"Bye. Bye."

"Bye. Bye."

Mrs Seow unlocked the front door and let herself in. She glanced at the clock. It was two fifteen in the morning. The light in the living room was on. So was the light in Yisheng's room. Strange, she thought to herself. Instead of heading for her own room, she went in the direction of Yisheng's room, handbag and a bag of supper in tow.

"Why aren't you in bed yet," she enquired of Yisheng.

Yisheng pointed at the bare floor space in front of the TV set.

"It's gone! That old man has taken it away," he sobbed.

Mrs Seow seemed prepared for such a situation. With the bag of supper still clutched in her left hand, she pointed at the wall behind Yisheng.

"Yesterday, that good-for-nothing (evidently Yisheng had taken this nickname for his father from his mother) came to my room and asked me for $300. I told him I didn't have any more money to give him and he stormed out of the house after quarrelling with me."

"I don't know why I married him. The Gods must be crazy to let me meet up with him in the first place."

By now, Mrs Seow had flown into a rage. She ignored the fact that it was already the wee hours of the morning. It didn't matter to her that everyone else was sleeping.

"That sorry-sight-of-a-man, your father, had better not come back or else I'll chase him out of the house. After all, this house is in my name."

She threw her handbag onto the settee and continued.

"Luckily, his name is not in the house's ownership papers, otherwise he would have sold the house too, and we would all be sleeping on the roadside."

Yisheng was sorry he had brought up the matter. He wanted his mother to stop the noise. He didn't want the neighbours to hear about his father. Deep down, he was sorry for his mother. He had no love for his father at all now. In fact, for the past few years, he had only thought of his father as the man who stayed with them and slept on the floor in the living room. – the man who, after learning he was working part-time at McDonald's, would plead with him for the little money he had earned. How he wished he hadn't such a father. Heaven was so unkind to him. How he wished that he could wake up and find it all a bad dream – a nightmare. But, he had awakened many times before, and nothing had changed. It was all real, alright. He couldn't change his fate.

The neighbour on the right had started to bang on the wall separating the two flats. Mrs Seow's voice fell to a low tone. She was still very angry, but it was her own business and nothing to do with the rest of the world. She knew at once she had to keep from making a racket at this ungodly hour.

"I'll change the locks to the front door tomorrow!" she declared.

With that statement, she pulled Yisheng into the living room and ripped open the paper bag she was holding. There were two meat *paus* and three *siew mai* in it. She flattened the opened paper bag and picked up a *pau* to give to Yisheng.

"Here. Eat this up. Forget about that useless idiot. We don't need him. You don't need a father. You've got me. We've got each other. That's enough."

There was no mention of Yisheng's father from that night on. There was also no mention of Yisheng's Nintendo set. Yisheng realised that he had to buy one himself if he wanted a Nintendo again.

Yisheng had forgotten about his Fire Disco and American Corner appointments. He was in no mood to go out to enjoy himself. He kept to the flat the next few days.

The end-of-year examinations were barely ten days away now and Yisheng had yet to begin work on his revisions. His teachers, particularly Mrs Trina Lee, were constantly breathing down his neck the last few days before the examinations. They said they were doing it for his own good. But, this young boy apparently didn't understand what that was all about – doing it for his own good.

The afternoons found Yisheng in his room at home, huddled next to his hi-fi set, with Kelvin and Simon as company. The trio was supposedly studying for the examinations, but, it was more a case of them engaging in chit-chat rather than revision talk. Still, it was better to have them indoors rather than out in the streets or shopping centres, loitering around.

Yisheng now had a new set of house keys. His mother had made good on her promise to replace the locks to the front door and grille gate. Apart from McDonald's and school, Yisheng did not go anywhere, not even to his favourite haunt at the coffeeshop. Both Kelvin and Simon did not insist on him going there either. They knew he was still upset over the loss of his Nintendo and somehow they could feel that Yisheng wanted to get into his mother's good books so that she would buy him another Nintendo set. It could be wishful thinking on his part, but Yisheng had to try his luck anyway.

So, you see, the way to get this young chap to study was to find a way to motivate him through dangling a carrot, such as an electronic gadget, in front of him. But, this time, the situation was a little weird. Nobody was dangling a carrot in front of Yisheng, yet he was trying to revise. It would be premature to describe his attempt at revision as bona fide, for he was never one to take to books readily. Still, things could turn out differently, and the teachers at school could be pleasantly surprised when the results came out.

The examinations came and went. There was still no sign of Yisheng's father. Nobody heard a thing about him those few weeks. He had apparently disappeared into thin air. What surprised Yisheng was that it was the first time in his life that he had actually studied for an examination, never mind that it was a sloppy effort at it. He didn't know how well or rather, how badly, he had fared in the examinations. He hoped that he could pass his English, Geography and Physical Science.

He had faith in his Maths. With Bulldog Ee around, he thought he would never have to worry about failing his Maths again. How could somebody he hated so much be a blessing in disguise to him, he thought. But, he never found out.

Yisheng learnt from the grapevine that a number of classmates had failed five subjects, and a handful had failed three subjects. He resigned himself to the thought that he was in either of the groups, and that his wish for a Nintendo set from his mother had been pulverised. When it was time to get back the examination answer papers for checking, Yisheng discovered that he had failed in Geography and Art. He had passed all his other subjects. It was a first for him at this school – the first time he failed only two subjects. It was indeed an achievement for him. He gloated over his results as he shared them with his pals, Kelvin and Simon.

Kelvin's results were a little better. He only failed in one subject, Physical Science. He was forever weak at Physical Science – anything to do with Science. Simon, on the other hand, had a pass in every subject. He didn't need pushing. He had a goal, and it was this goal which had spurred him on. He wanted to become an engineer, to leave the house and settle on his own. He wanted to be free from his father's clutches. As to why he harboured this desire, only Kelvin and Yisheng knew. Simon, like Yisheng, came from a broken home. He lived in a five-room flat in a Block 229 with his family. His father was two-timing his mother. He had a mistress outside and came home infrequently. Whenever he was home, there would be heated arguments between husband and wife, and Simon and his two brothers could feel the bad vibes in their home constantly. It would a few more years before Simon would be free of this pressure-cooker situation. He was enduring it as best he could. His two younger brothers were too young to understand, they being at least five years younger than him.

The three boys, walking abreast, headed towards the school gates. It was the last day of school for them that year. It was a half-day session, from 7.20 am to 9.30 am. They had collected their report books from their form teacher earlier in the morning and when the bell rang for dismissal, the three of them had gathered at the staircase landing before moving down the stairs. Now, they were about to approach the school gates, and once past that metal thing, they had nothing to do with school till 3 January 1989, which was two long months away.

"Yippee!"

They shouted as they dashed across the road, and strolled to their favourite *mama-shop*. Kelvin had reason to rejoice. Come next week, he would be fifteen years old exactly, and he could start work legally at McDonald's. He could join Simon and Yisheng at work at McDonald's Marina Square instead of watching them work from the customers' seating area outside the counter. Simon could only think of the money he would be earning at McDonald's that holiday season. Of course, his mind was also on the sweet girls that would come by the fast-food restaurant every day – it was holiday season after all and all these pretty gals would be hanging around the shopping centres.

As for Yisheng, he was still thinking about his chances of getting a Nintendo from his mother before Christmas. He had to get one before Christmas. He remembered his mother had promised to get him a motorcycle for his birthday at the end of January 1989. He was sure his mother would not get both things for him at the same time. He had to be careful not to make his mother angry over little things the next few weeks so he was, alas, on his best behaviour, at least till he got his Nintendo. But whether he would get his Nintendo and the Honda scrambler was quite another story. It remained to be seen.

Use of Singlish and other non-English phrases in the book

The author has used only a smattering of commonly used Singlish terms such as *wah, lah, aiyah, heng-ah* and *alamak* in the book.

Ah Lian	:	street-wise girl or woman
Ah Sohs	:	aunties
Angmoh	:	Caucasian
Aiyah	:	a moaning sound uttered to express regret
Aiyoh	:	similar to 'aiyah'
Alamak	:	similar in meaning to 'alas'
Ang Pow	:	red packet/envelope containing cash
Chiak bak	:	gain an advantage
Heng-ah	:	similar in meaning to 'luckily'
Kakees	:	buddies
Kiasu	:	scared of losing out to others; afraid of making mistakes
Kway teow	:	flat rice vermicelli noodles, but in this book, phrase is used to denote caning
Lah	:	added to the end of a sentence for positive emphasis
Layang	:	kite
Lor	:	added to the end of a sentence for emphasis
Mama-shop	:	kiosk selling provisions
Mata-putehs	:	small singing birds with white eyes
Pau	:	Chinese bun with fillings such as meat or bean paste
Siew Mai	:	Chinese dumpling with fillings such as pork or shrimp
Wah	:	similar in meaning to 'wow'

Novel by the Author

Mystery of the Battle Box

The 290-page story is partly set in Greendale Secondary School and Hougang housing estate in Singapore.

Jing Yang, his classmate Angelina, and his cousin Tim team up to solve a mystery about hidden treasure in an underground bunker which was built during World War Two.

A history dropout from a local university has been searching for the treasure for many years. The teenagers must find the treasure first before he does.

They stumble into a secret tunnel beneath the bunker with help from two spirits haunting the bunker since World War Two.

Just when they lay eyes on the gold bars hidden in the secret tunnel, who else but the history dropout should turn up behind them, startling them and causing a sudden turn of events...

Cover illustration by Raymond Han

Visit the author's Web site

Find out more about Raymond Han on his Web site at www.raymondhan.net.